MURDER FEST KEY WEST

BY

MAC FORTNER

Mac Fortner

CAM DERRINGER SERIES:

BOOK 4

DEDICATION

This is for all the men and women who work to keep our country out of harm's way. Without them, the streets wouldn't be safe to walk. Some feel they aren't safe now, but can you imagine how bad it would be if not for the bravery of our armed forces and our police departments? When you pass one such person on the street, thank them. They do it for you.

Don't miss the other exciting books in this series:

KNEE DEEP–BOOK 1

BLOODSHOT–BOOK 2

KEY WEST: TWO BIRDS ONE STONE–BOOK 3

OTHER BOOKS BY MAC FORTNER:

SUNNY RAY SERIES:

RUM CITY BAR

BATTLE FOR RUMORA

These books can be found on Amazon

AND GET THE <u>FREE</u> PREQUEL TO THE

CAM DERRINGER SERIES:

A DARK NIGHT IN KEY WEST

<u>HERE</u>

<u>https://bit.ly/2JRAFEX</u>

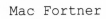

Mac Fortner

Prologue

The rain had let up slightly. Karen sat in a booth next to the window where she could watch the storm and yet be sheltered from the torrent of on again off again gusts of wind and rain.

She killed time reading the names, and words of wisdom, that had been carved into the rough, but varnished wooden tabletop.

A young girl about her age sat down across from her in the booth. Karen looked up at her and then took a quick glance around the room. The bar was empty except for the two of them.

"Hi," the girl said, offering a bright smile. "Mind if I join you?"

"Sure," Karen said.

"My name's Tracy," the girl said extending her hand.

"Karen," she said shaking Tracy's hand.

Tracy held Karen's hand lightly but firm enough to keep it in hers.

"Nice to meet you," Tracy said.

Karen nodded, taking a look at their hands and then back at Tracy.

Tracy moved her hand to the table, resting it there but still holding Karen's.

"Waiting the rain out?" Tracy asked.

"Yeah, it's terrible," Karen said looking out the window.

"It's not going to get any drier out there," Tracy said.

"No, probably not."

They still held hands, making Karen a little uncomfortable.

"You on vacation?" Tracy asked.

"Working vacation. Murder Fest Key West."

"Oh, you're an author."

"Editor," Karen said.

Tracy squeezed her hand. "Sounds exciting."

"Not really, but I am going to write a book someday."

"Great, where are you stayin'?" Tracy probed.

"The Orchid Field Inn, on Whitehead Street," she said. "I always wanted to stay at a B&B so I booked that instead of the Caribbean Palm Village Resort where everyone else is."

"Listen," Tracy said. "I work here and I have a room upstairs. Why don't you spend the night here and go home tomorrow after the storm."

"I don't think so," Karen said pulling her hand away. "I need to get back to my room and do some work."

"I'll make it worth your while," Tracy said smiling and parting her lips slightly.

"Thanks anyway," Karen said apologetically.

"Okay, your loss," Tracy said flatly and stood. "See you around."

Karen smiled to herself. *My first lesbian encounter. I wonder what it would be like?*

The rain has slacked and it seems to be Karen's best chance of getting to her B&B without getting soaked. She signaled for the waiter to bring her bill. Thirty-four dollars for two beers and a nacho plate. *Ridiculous,* she thought. Food, actually everything, was much more reasonable in Paris, Illinois.

It was a turn of fate when her name was drawn randomly from the forty-five editors in her category. The young woman who delivered the ticket to her took her totally by surprise. She didn't even know there *was* a contest to come to the Murder Fest Key West.

She needed a break from her boyfriend and his increasingly violent temper. It was time to break it off with him before he hurt her too badly.

Looking out the window again, she could see the storefronts across the street. Most were closed to keep the rain from soaking the knick-knacks that were displayed at the entrances.

Her thoughts returned to her *lovely life.*

Her mother's new husband had been a problem too. He can't keep his hands to himself. Out of the three stepfathers she's had, he was by far the worst.

Turning twenty-five three days ago, she knew it was time to leave anyway. *I'll move to Indiana and get my own place in Terre Haute when I get back home.*

Opening the door to leave, a sheet of wind and water hit her in the face temporarily blinding her. *Not as calm as I thought.* She braced herself and pushed through the door and onto the sidewalk. Turning left, she hurried her pace from awning to awning along the storefronts. They didn't offer much protection. The rain was running down her neck and soaking her back under the light windbreaker she wore. She paused at an open door leading to the stairs for a second-floor bar.

Using the portico for protection, she unzipped her collar and pulled the hood out. *What the hell. From now on, I'm going to live my life to the fullest. I'll make it full of firsts.*

The streets were almost deserted. *I guess everyone else got the memo.* A few brave souls were still barhopping along Duval Street. The rain didn't seem to deter their spirits any. They were laughing while running from one bar to the next.

Karen stepped from the doorway, held her arms out and spun around twice. She laughed and ran down the sidewalk.

She turned down a side street. It was a short-cut to her B&B. The buildings were now offering some protection from the storm.

"Hey there," she heard a voice say.

She started and turned toward the voice.

She could barely make out a figure in the shadow of a large Banyan tree.

"Yes," she said. "Can I help you?"

"Hi, Karen."

Karen strained to see the stranger. When the figure stepped from beneath the tree, Karen said, "Oh, it's you."

Maria Martinez unsnapped the latch on her purse and pulled her keys out. It was still a little dark outside from the lingering clouds left by the storm last night. She and Eduardo closed the shop early the night before, knowing there would be no customers in a storm like that.

She strained her eyes to choose the right key to the shop door. That's when her foot hit something on the sidewalk and she fell landing softly as if on a cushion.

It took a few seconds for her eyes to focus on what was only inches from her face. When they did, she wished that they hadn't. There were foggy eyes staring back at her. Not exactly staring I guess. That would imply they were actually seeing something.

Maria screamed. No sound at first, but the momentum built until an ear-piercing pitch erupted from deep in her throat.

She put her hand to her mouth to stop the noise from within. That's when she felt something slimy and thick on her hand and now on her face.

Pulling her hand away and holding it up to see, she saw what was undeniably blood, a lot of blood. She screamed again and tried to get to her feet without touching the body lying under her. It was impossible. She was sliding in more blood. Finally, she rolled away and got to her feet. She ran a few steps and slipped again, almost falling. Blood was everywhere.

She ran into the street and just missed being struck by a man on a bicycle. He swerved and stopped sliding sideways.

"Damn it, lady," he yelled before seeing her face and then her clothes. "Are you okay?"

Murder Fest Key West

Chapter 1

Cowboy and the Blonde

I was having a drink down at Sloppy Joes with Jack when I noticed a dame enter the saloon. She was a tall blonde with a shapely figure. She looked like probably the type who could handle herself and anyone else that got in her way.

I stopped writing. I couldn't think of what to say next. My first attempt at writing a novel and I developed writer's block after only three sentences–forty-six words.

I had better stick with being a PI. At least I never lack for something clever to say.

I was spirited into the world of writing by a friend of mine from college, Cody Paxton, who is coming to Key West tomorrow for Murder Fest Key West. It's an annual celebration of the best mystery writers and crime experts in the world.

Cody's the bestselling author of fifteen mystery/suspense novels. I've invited him to stay with me on my boat. I thought maybe I could impress him with my literary skills. I even visited Hemmingway's house to get inspired.

Evidently, writing isn't for everyone. I don't mind, really. What little I did write took me thirty minutes. I figured a novel could take up at least a year of my life.

I closed out the word app on my computer and Googled Cody Paxton again.

There were pictures of him accepting various writing awards in fancy banquet rooms. They were neatly arranged in chronological order. Each picture showed Cody in a different era of his life. The eyes seemed to lose a little of their light and the lids slowly covered more of the eye itself. His face filled out and waistline grew a bit.

He was still a handsome man but not exactly a heart-throb. Thank God I hadn't aged any since the days we shared a dorm room at Yale.

My cell phone rang. I checked the caller ID. It was from the Key West Police Department. Probably wanting another donation.

"Hello," I said reluctantly.

"Cam?"

"Yes."

"This is Chief Leland."

"Chief, how are you?" I said.

I worked with the Chief a few months ago when a young lady was trying to persuade the justice system to lock me away for the rest of my life. Luckily, we came out the victors in that case.

"I'm fine Cam, but I've got someone in my cell who says he's a friend of yours. He was a little intoxicated when we stopped him a few hours ago for driving on the wrong side of Roosevelt Boulevard. If he wasn't your friend I'd let him stay. We'd just gag him."

"What's his name?"

"Cody Paxton."

It didn't take Cody long to pick up where he left off the last time I saw him. Late in the evening after our graduation ceremony, Cody threw a wine bottle through a window in the Paxton House, a women's dorm that was named after his grandfather who donated the funds to build it. I ran, he didn't. I picked him up the next morning at the police station. His parents paid for the window and the statue, which was on the desk next to the window. The college was more than cooperative and didn't file charges once they realized who he was.

"Yes, he is a friend of mine. He'll be staying with me during the writer's convention. May I come and pick him up?"

"Normally, no, but in this case, please do. I can't take any more of his singing."

"Ah, yes. I remember—very loud and off-key."

"Please hurry."

"I'm on my way."

I tried to hide the shock that was bound to show on my face when I saw Cody. His six-foot-two muscular frame was now closer to six foot and pudgy. He had at least a four-day growth of whiskers on his face and his hair was—for the lack of a better word–a mess. No matter how much you Google someone and study their pictures, it doesn't prepare you for the real thing.

Reunions with old friends are never what you expect them to be. I knew what he was looking at also. A much older Cam Derringer. A little grey around the temples, larger stature. Muscles had filled in the skinny college boy physique. A little of the shine absent from my eyes also.

"Cam my man," he yelled loud enough to wake the dead.

"Hello, Cody. I see you arrived a little early."

"Yes, indeed I did. Does it always rain this hard here?"

"No."

The duty officer gave me a bag of Cody's personal possessions and told us we were free to go. We could pick his car up from impound tomorrow morning.

"Just don't let him drive," the officer said.

I took Cody by the arm and steered him through the door and to my car. His suit was still wet from the rain. Once we were settled inside, he shook my hand.

"Great to see you again, Cam," he said slightly slurring his words.

"You too, Cody," I said. "It's been a long time."

"Hey, let's stop and get a beer before we go home," he said.

"Not tonight," I said. "Let's go to my place and have a drink."

"That sounds even better."

We arrived at my dock and I parked the car.

"What are we doing here?" he asked.

"This is where I live."

"You live under the dock?"

"On a boat."

He looked around the docks. "I hope it's that big Navy vessel over there," he said pointing at my boat.

"It is," I said.

He looked at me, his mouth open wide.

"No," he said.

"Yep."

He reached for the door handle.

"Wait a minute and I'll come around and help you," I said.

"I can make it," he said and opened the door.

He didn't make it. He fell out and onto the parking lot. His feet were still in the car and the rain was pounding him in the face.

"Help, I'm drowning," he said laughing.

I couldn't lift him back in the car so I drug him the rest of the way out and got him to his feet.

"Don't tell anyone about that," he said. "My reputation would be blemished."

"Don't worry. I don't think we can hurt your reputation."

"Thank you."

"Let's get to the boat. We're getting soaked out here."

I led him through the gate and down the dock. We walked up the gangway and onto the deck.

I opened the sliding door and led him inside.

"Son of a bitch, Cam. Did you steal this," he said looking at the interior of the boat.

"No, actually, it was a gift from a friend."

"A girl I bet."

"Have a seat," I said pointing at the sofa.

He ignored me.

"What would you like to drink?"

This got his attention.

I poured us two Wild Turkeys and handed him one.

"You're still on the Turkey, eh," he said.

"I've never found anything that I like better."

He drank it down in one big gulp. I had expected us to sip for a while as we caught up on old times.

He set his empty glass on the coffee table and sat on the sofa.

"How's your writing going?" I asked.

He fell over on his side and closed his eyes.

I was glad he did. It really wasn't much fun talking to him in his current condition. Tomorrow we would catch up.

I removed his wet coat, got a blanket from the closet and covered him.

I called Diane and let her know Cody was here.

"Really? I thought he wouldn't be here until tomorrow," she said.

"He surprised me."

"Let me talk to him," she said.

"He's tired and went to bed."

"Tell him I'll see him tomorrow then."

"I will."

"Goodnight Dad."

"Goodnight baby."

I thought about Diane seeing Cody tomorrow. I hoped he would be in better form. Her being a psychiatrist might turn out to be a good thing.

Chapter 2

I woke early the next morning and quietly made my way to the shower. After I dressed, I went into the living room to check on my guest.

He wasn't there. I could smell the coffee. I poured a cup and went to the front lanai. He was sitting at the table writing. I watched for a moment before I said anything. Maybe he was writing a new bestseller right here on my boat.

"Good morning," I said.

He started and turned. "Good morning, Cam. I was just leaving you a note."

"A note?"

"Yes, I was going to the impound to pick up my car."

"How were you even going to get there?"

"I have an Uber app on my phone."

"You know I was planning to take you to get it."

"I didn't want to put you out," he said sheepishly. "After last night I figured you might be glad to get rid of me."

"Not at all, Cody. That wasn't the first time I had to pick you up off the street," I said and chuckled.

"You had to pick me up off the street?"

"You had a little trouble getting out of the car."

"Sorry about that. I only had a couple of beers."

"Why don't you get in the shower and shave. By the time you get out, I'll have breakfast ready."

"That does sound good. I don't want you to go to a lot of trouble for me though."

"No trouble, Cody."

I showed him to the bathroom and got him a towel. I laid out some clothes that were a little tight on me. I knew they weren't going to be perfect but they had to be better than the wet, *blood-stained* suit he was wearing.

Where'd the blood come from? Maybe he hurt himself when he fell out of the car.

I went to the galley and started on breakfast. I put the bacon on to fry while I mixed the pancake batter. When the bacon finished I removed it and placed it on a covered plate, broke some eggs and dropped them in the bacon grease. That should be good for a hangover. Although, he didn't seem to have one. Maybe he's used to waking in that condition.

When he walked into the galley, he looked like a new man. His hair was neat and the clothes seemed to fit. Maybe a little large but not bad.

"Are you okay?" I asked.

"I feel great and that food smells delicious."

"Eat up," I said. "I can fix more if you need it."

"This will be fine. I don't eat much," he said as he started in on his first helping.

After I repeated the breakfast prep for the second time and he ate half of that too, he pushed himself away from the table.

"I was hungrier than I thought," he said.

"Me too," I said even though I only ate one pancake and a piece of bacon.

"Are you cut anywhere?"

"Cut?"

"Yeah, there was some blood on your suit coat."

"I don't think so. I didn't notice anything."

"I'll ask Diane what to use to get it out."

"Diane. Will she be coming to see me?"

"Yeah, I called her last night. She wants to see you today."

"Great, I can finally put a face to the voice."

"It's a very pretty face."

"I bet it is."

"When did you last speak with her?"

"Last year. I had some questions concerning psychiatry for my new book."

"How's it going, the book?" I asked.

"I released it three months ago. I've had better."

"All your others hit number one right away," I said.

"Yes, I've been lucky."

"Luck has nothing to do with it. I've read a few of your books. I love them."

"Thanks for that. It means a lot coming from you. I actually brought you a signed copy of my new one."

"Let's have it then."

"It's in my car."

"Speaking of which, we should go get it."

"I'm ready if you are."

"I tried to write a book last week," I said. "After one page I realized I would be working for about a nickel a day. How do you make your books best-sellers?"

"I start out with a bang. I always kill someone off in the prologue. People love murder and suspense."

"I think that's my problem. I didn't want anyone to die."

"Ya' gotta kill 'em, Cam."

We drove to the lot located behind the Police Station. Cody's car was sitting in the front row.

I asked the attendant if Chief Leland was around.

"No, there was a murder last night. Some young girl got herself killed," he said.

"A local?"

"Don't know. He just got a call this morning, came in here, took a car and left," the attendant said.

"Do you know where?"

"Whitehead Street a block off Duval."

"Thanks," I said.

"Okay Cody, your car is ready to go. I'm going to the crime scene to see if I can help," I told him.

"I wanna go too. There might be a story in it," he said.

"Okay, but you have to stay back. The Chief doesn't like people trampling his crime scene."

"No problem."

As soon as we turned onto Whitehead Street, we saw a mass of blue lights flashing. Barricades had been set up, so we parked the car behind the last police cruiser and walked. We were stopped short of the scene by an officer.

"You'll have to stay back here," he said not even giving us a glance. He already had a crowd of onlookers who were eager to see what would undoubtedly haunt them in their dreams tonight.

"Good morning, Mike," I said.

15

He looked at me. "Cam," he said. "Come on in but watch where you step. It's a mess. Leland's over there," he said pointing toward a small group standing around a covered figure on the ground.

We went under the crime tape and toward Leland. I stopped after a few steps and asked Cody to wait here.

"Alright," he said not protesting.

"Morning Chief," I said.

"Cam."

"What do we have?"

"Carnage."

I looked down at the covered corps. There was plenty of blood. Whatever was under that tarp wasn't going anywhere.

The body was lying in a doorway half hidden from the street. If not for the heavy rain last night and the lack of people on the street, this could not have occurred right out in the open as it did.

"Do you have an ID?" I asked.

"Tammy Decker, age twenty-five, from Sebree, Kentucky."

"How did it happen?"

"You have to keep this to yourself," Leland said. "Someone cut her heart out through her back. It was in a grocery bag hanging on the doorknob there," and pointed at the door next to the body.

We stood in silence, staring blankly.

Chapter 3

When we were back in the car, Cody asked what happened.

"A tourist was stabbed in the back."

"Male or female?"

"Female."

"Young or old?"

"Young."

"What else can you tell me?"

"Nothing."

"Come on Cam, you gotta give me something."

I knew I didn't have to give him anything and it made me feel disloyal, kind of, to hold back.

"They don't know anything else yet," I said.

"I can make a book out of that. If you learn anything else let me know. Okay?"

"If I can, I will."

We drove back to the impound and picked up Cody's car. He followed me back to the boat.

When we arrived, Cody excused himself. He returned to the lanai with pen and paper in hand.

"I need to make a few notes," he said.

"That's fine."

"I was inspired by the crime scene a while ago. When I see something like that my mind starts writing and if I don't jot down the details I'll lose 'em."

"I can understand that," I said.

Now I know I wouldn't make a good writer. I can't think about making a story out of a tragedy. I can only think of the unfortunate victim. If he knew her heart was cut out through her back, he would be ecstatic.

It was another beautiful, muggy day since the rain had stopped. I decided to go for a run. I asked Cody if he'd like to join me. I'd be running alone.

I ran my usual route. When I passed the Caribbean Palm Village Resort, I saw "Welcome Writers" on the marque. The convention would be starting tomorrow. Cody has invited me to attend the opening with him. It might be interesting.

I ran to Smathers Beach and along Roosevelt to First Street, turned right and ran toward Garrison Bight. I didn't have a destination in mind today. I just wanted to run the image of that poor girl out of my mind.

I paused at North Roosevelt waiting for traffic to stop. Then I crossed and ran along the harbor where the palm trees lined the walkway. When I turned right again on Eisenhower Drive, I realized I did have a destination in mind. My sometimes partner and good friend Jack Stiller ran a charter fishing business out of Garrison Bight Marina.

I saw him hosing off his boat. He probably had already taken a group of tourist out this morning.

"Hey, Jack," I greeted.

"Hey, Cam," he answered.

Gomer Pyle started a whole new language for saying, "Hi."

"What brings you all the way down here this morning?" he asked.

"I needed to burn some memories."

"Bad, huh."

"Yeah," I said and told him the whole story about the crime scene.

"That's a bad one."

"I know. The vision won't go away."

"You need some help with it?"

"Probably."

"I'm free the rest of the day," he said.

"I'm going to check back with Leland in a few hours to see what has developed. I'll call you then," I said.

I didn't really have any idea what to do right now. I was just killing time until….until what?

"I'm going to run down to Whitehead Street and try to find someone that might have seen something," I said.

"Give me a minute and I'll run with you," Jack said.

"Good, I could use the company."

When Jack returned I felt a little inadequate. His six-foot-five muscular frame was eighteen years younger than mine. Though he was only one inch taller than I was, it seemed like a foot.

We ran through old town dodging in and out of the heavy traffic. When we came to Whitehead Street, we turned left and ran to Amelia Street.

The crime scene tape was still in place around the doorway where Tammy was found. There was a bench on the sidewalk so we sat and caught our breath. From the bench, we had a good view of the surrounding area. The weather was sunny and humid, around eighty-five degrees. You would never know there was a storm here last night dropping three inches of rain.

"You would think someone would have seen something," I said.

"You would think," Jack said. "But it was raining hard and the streets were empty."

"I don't see any street cameras," I said looking around.

Jack took a look too. "No."

I noticed a young woman watching us from a second-floor window in a B&B across the street. I waved at her slightly. She retreated into her room.

"I'm going to try to talk to her," I said.

"I'll stay down here," Jack said.

I went to the office of the B&B. The receptionist sat behind an undersized wooden desk. She looked as if she were playing school. She eyed me uneasily. I asked her for the name of the woman on the second floor facing Whitehead Street. She just stared at me. It wasn't a friendly look.

I flashed my P.I. badge.

"I know who you are, *Mister Derringer*," she emphasized the name through gritted teeth.

"I'm sorry," I said. "Have I offended you in some way?"

"Pete Daily," she hissed.

The name seemed familiar to me. I sifted through my mental Rolodex and finally came up with the name, *ooh ooh.*

Pete was in the middle of robbing a street food vendor about six years ago when I happened along. He had a gun pointed at the man. I snuck up from behind and grabbed the gun. Pete wasn't willing to give it up so easily. With his heightened state of mind and strength from the meth he was on, we fought. The gun went off and Pete was killed. I was cleared by the court with the testimony of the street vendor.

"You're Pete's friend?" I said.

"Sister."

"Sorry that happened, but he was going to kill that man."

"I doubt it, but that's what your friend said in court," she said sarcastically.

"He wasn't my friend. I didn't even know him."

"Hum," she said sharply. "Anyway, you can't go to her room. It's private."

I left and returned to Jack. He was talking to a man in an apron.

"Cam, this is Eduardo Martinez. He owns the shop where the girl was found."

Eduardo extended his hand. We shook.

"Are you the one who found the body?" I asked.

"No, no my wife," he said.

"About what time was that?"

"Five-thirty or so this morning," he said thoughtfully "I don't guess she saw anyone else around."

"No. She didn't see the girl until she stepped into the doorway. The body was hidden by the walls of the building."

"Were you here last night?" I asked.

"No, we close early." He looked at the sky and held his hands out. "Rain."

"Okay. Thank you for your time."

"You are welcome," Eduardo said.

"How did it go with the girl in the window?" Jack asked.

"I didn't get to see her. I killed the receptionist's brother."

Jack just looked at me and shook his head. He's known me long enough that nothing surprises him.

My cell phone rang. It was Chief Leland.

"Good afternoon, Chief," I said.

"Afternoon, Cam. There's been another murder."

"Already?"

"Yep, same MO."

Chapter 4

Jack and I called a taxi and arrived at the Key West International Airport twenty-five minutes later. More Police cruisers and yellow tape. I thought briefly, about how many times I've arrived at the same scene, just different locations.

"Chief," I said again.

"Cam, Jack," he answered back.

"What now?" I asked.

"More of the same. This time it's a young man. A passerby saw him lying in the back seat of his car. Tony Baxter twenty-six from Nashville, Tennessee."

"Nashville," I said thoughtfully.

"Yep, Tammy and now Tony."

"Did they know each other?" Jack asked.

"Don't know. Sebree is only sixteen-hundred population. I googled it. It's two and a half hours from Nashville."

"His heart?" I said.

"In a grocery bag hanging from the hanger hook."

"Time of death?"

"Last night as far as we can tell. During the rainstorm."

"Someone was busy last night," I said. "I wonder if it was a jealous boyfriend?"

"Or wife," Leland said. "Tony's married."

I looked at the corpse and felt sympathy for his family. Wrong place at the wrong time? I hoped so.

"There is one thing we know about him. He was here for the writer's convention."

"He was?"

"There was a book in his car, with him featured as the author."

"I guess the rain washed away all the evidence here too."

"It looks like it. There's nothing to go on yet. Jackson's checking the security cams. Hopefully, they picked something up," Leland said.

As if on cue, his cell phone rang. He listened, "Okay, thanks," he said.

"Well, the storm killed the cameras last night. We didn't get anything," he said.

"Have you talked to Tammy's parents yet?" I asked.

"No, I was getting ready for that when this came in."

"Maybe it would be best to ask *them* if they know Tony, instead of the other way around. I know both families will discover what happened, but no sense starting something beforehand."

"Yeah, I guess, but sooner or later I'm going to have to ask Tony's wife if she knows Tammy."

"I'll ask Cody if he knows Tony Baxter. Maybe we can find a connection between the two. I'll want to talk to anyone else that knew him too. I'm going to the opening ceremony at the Key West Murder Fest with Cody. That'll give me an opportunity."

"Good," the chief said. "Let me know what you find out."

The sun was directly overhead now and the heat was once again unbearable. The officers surrounding the car were soaked. It was from the heat, not the rain. No one was talking and joking as they sometimes do at crime scenes. The two murders today seemed to hit them hard.

"Are we running or calling a cab?" I asked Jack.

"I'm taking a taxi. You can do what you please," he said.

"I don't want you to get lonesome," I said. "I'll ride with you."

Jack came back to the boat with me to talk to Cody.

We found him still sitting on the lanai writing. He now had his laptop open and was completely engrossed in his thoughts.

"Hey, Cody," I said.

He jumped and grabbed his chest.

"Don't do that," he said. "You could give me a heart attack."

"Sorry," I said and then introduced Jack.

They shook hands and exchanged pleasantries.

"Have you finished the book you started this morning?" I joked.

"Not quite, but I do have an outline."

"Well, I've got a new plot for ya."

"Really?" He said, his face lit up and he grinned.

"There was another murder."

"Same MO?"

"Yep."

"Another girl?"

25

"Nope."

"A man?"

"Do you really have to ask that?" I said.

"Who and where?

"They found him in his car in the airport parking lot. You might know him. I hope not."

"Who is it," he said, now more somber.

"Tony Baxter," I said.

His face dropped. He looked thoughtful and puzzled.

"Did you say, Tony Baxter?"

"Yes. Why? Do you know him?"

He was silent for a moment and then, "The girl they found this morning, was there something very unusual about the way she was killed?"

"Maybe?" I said.

"Her name Tammy Decker?"

"Yes."

Cody turned white.

"What is it, Cody?" Jack said.

"I want to show you something," he said and stood.

He went inside and returned with one of his paperbacks.

"Read the back," he said.

I looked at the cover first. The title was bold and went right through me.

TRADING HEARTS a Colt Grey Novel, Book One

I turned the book over and read the description.

Tony Baxter lost his heart. Tammy found it. An unexpected gift hanging on her doorknob. She learns she must give her heart to him in order to solve the conundrum known only as, Fair Exchange, and save her family from a death more intense than Hell itself.

It went on but I quit reading and looked at Cody. I handed the book to Jack.

"What the hell is that?" I said.

"Your man's name isn't Tony Baxter," Cody said. "Their hearts were cut out through their backs, weren't they."

"What else do you know?" I said now in a partial trance.

"Those aren't their hearts," he said. "They are, but they're switched."

Chapter 5

I picked up the bottle of Wild Tukey sitting on the patio bar and poured myself a healthy shot. I drank it down in one gulp and poured another. This one I sipped.

Jack picked up the bottle and did the same. Cody looked at the bottle but didn't move.

"When did you write this book?" I asked.

"Three years ago. I've sold around a hundred-thousand copies."

"But this guy, Tony, he had books in his car with his name on them. He was the author," Jack said.

"Yeah, sounds right. Tony Baxter is an author from Nashville, Tennessee. I made him up. It's not that hard to have a name switched on a book."

We were silent again for a few minutes.

"Am I missing something here?"

"Not if you think my book has come alive," Cody said. "Someone is copying 'Trading Hearts'"

"Any ideas about who or why or even how?"

"Yeah, maybe, but you're not going to like it."

"Try me," I said.

"In the book, there was an author who actually wrote the book TRADING HEARTS. His name was Tony Baxter. Tony's girlfriend committed the murders in order for his book to become a bestseller. In the end, Tony cut her heart out and put it in a jar so their hearts would remain close together. He would sleep with it."

"Where did you come up with such a gruesome story?"

"That's the way my mind works. I can't help it."

I downed my whiskey and poured another. Cody looked at the bottle again but didn't reach for it.

"You know the police are going to want to question you about this, don't you."

"I would think so. They did in my book," Cody said.

"The police questioned Tony?" I said.

"Yeah, Cam, you do know it was just a book of fiction, don't you?"

"Yes, I get that, but now it's all too real. Who would do such a thing?"

"You've got me. I don't have the slightest idea."

I thought for a moment.

"Okay, so you wrote a book about another author who wrote the book, 'Trading Hearts.' Right?"

"Right."

"The author's girlfriend in your book was the one killing everyone. Right?"

"Right again."

"But you're actually the author who wrote, 'Trading Hearts.' Right?"

"You're making this way too complicated, Cam. I write books about people getting killed all the time. That doesn't mean I actually killed them."

"Yeah, Yeah, I know. I'm just trying to follow it."

My cell phone rang. I checked the caller ID. It was Diane.

"Hello, sweetie," I said, trying to be cheerful.

"Okay, see you then," I said.

I told them Diane was on her way over. Jack was delighted since they were dating.

"Why don't we keep this to ourselves for a while," I said.

"My lips are sealed," Cody said.

"I should call Leland before he tries to contact their families," I said. "Then we need to find out who they really are."

I called the chief and explained the best I could.

"Check blood types or DNA to see if the hearts were swapped," I said.

"If this is true Cam, I need to talk to Cody," he said.

"Yeah, we already figured that."

"I'll call you back when we get the results."

"Thanks, Chief."

I sat and thumbed through the paperback. Cody's warped. If it were any other time I would probably think this was a good read. But now, it's like reading a crime report.

"Hi guys," Diane said.

We didn't hear her come onto the boat. I don't know how we missed her though. You could hear a pin drop on the lanai.

Jack rose and hugged her. I did the same and gave her a light kiss on the cheek.

"Why all the gloomy faces when I came aboard?" she said.

"We were just relaxing," I said. "I'm reading one of Cody's new books, and speaking of the devil."

Cody stood.

"This is my beautiful daughter Diane. Diane this is Cody."

They hugged. "Cam said you were gorgeous, but I had no idea."

"Okay you guys," she said "Enough with the gorgeous stuff. It's nice to finally meet you, Cody."

"And you too," he said.

"Maybe you can tell me some old stories about Cam in his wilder days," she said.

"What you see is what you get. This is about as wild as he ever was."

"Yeah, right," she said.

"Maybe I can come up with one or two."

"Don't believe anything he says Diane, he's a storyteller. He makes it up as he goes."

Diane laughed at that, but Jack, Cody and I exchanged uneasy glances.

"What's going on?" Diane said. "You guys are hiding something."

"Did I tell you she was a shrink?" I said.

"Yeah, and I take it a good one," Cody said.

"We're working on a double homicide," I said. "Cody's helping us with some theories."

"Anything I can do?" She asked.

"Yeah," Jack said, "You can come inside with me and help get the steaks ready to grill."

"You got it," she said.

"Okay, you two, no fooling around in there," I said.

31

I don't like the idea that Jack and Diane are dating. I guess because I've known Jack for too long. He has a checkered past with the women. But Diane is a strong woman and I know she has a good head on her shoulders. I should trust them, but she's my everything. I can't help but be protective.

"Hello."

I turned to see Stacy, our neighbor who lives on the first houseboat as you come onto the dock. She's in her late twenties and hot. She was wearing her usual micro-bikini. She was holding a Brown Lab puppy.

"Who's that," I said.

"This is Hank," she said kissing him. "Hank, this is Cam. Beware, he'll only get you in trouble."

I reached out and petted Hank. He licked me.

"When did you get him?"

"This morning. After you had Walter here I realized I wanted a dog of my own."

Walter was a Golden Retriever I was babysitting for a friend. The darn dog ended up saving my life. Now seeing Hank, I missed Walter.

"Come on in and have a drink," I said.

She obliged.

"Stacy, this is Cody Paxton, an old friend of mine from college."

Cody stood and shook her hand. He didn't release it.

"Cody Paxton, like the author?" she said.

"Yes," he said. "You've heard of me?"

"Are you kiddin', I've got all your books."

"So, you're the one, huh."

She laughed, "Me and a million others."

"Have a seat," he said pulling out a chair next to his.

"Watch out for him, Stacy. He has a reputation," I said.

"I don't care," she said and sat down.

We had drinks and made small talk. Cody promised to sign her books before he left.

Jack and Diane appeared with some appetizers and a bottle of wine. Diane loved on Hank while I lit the Green Egg grill.

We had a pleasant evening and nothing else was said about the murders.

Chapter 6

Rick Johnson left his hotel room at ten P.M. and went to the parking lot. He saw his friend loading the fishing poles in the trunk of his car and approached.

"Hey Rick, you ready to catch some?" his friend said.

"Hell yes," Rick said.

They drove to the White Street Pier, parked and walked out to the railing. They were the only two on the pier tonight.

Rick pulled the line through the eyes on his pole and rigged the end with four hooks. He reached into the bait bucket and pulled out a chunk of fish and strung it carefully on the hook so it wouldn't come loose. He repeated the process for the other three hooks.

He was so engrossed with what he was doing he didn't notice the new figure arrive. Nor did he see his friend swing the rod that caught him on the back of the head.

~***~

When I went to bed that night I took Cody's book with me. Maybe I would gain some insight into what was going to happen next.

That was a big mistake. When I finally fell asleep, I had bad dreams all night. I woke to feel as if I'd been in a wreck.

I was drinking coffee in the living room when Hank came wandering in from the second bedroom. The one I gave Cody.

"Good morning Hank," I said.

He licked me. I decided to take him for a walk before he desecrated my boat.

I wasn't happy that Stacy spent the night with Cody. I expected them to have a little more respect for me. Stacy's boat is only fifty yards away. They could go there if they needed to be together.

We walked to the end of the dock before he paused and squatted. Luckily, he only had to do number one. I forgot to bring a bag with me.

"I told you to watch out for him, Hank," I heard Stacy say from behind us.

She held up a bag. "He was going to let you get in trouble."

"Sorry," I said. "I forgot it."

"Thanks for walking him," Stacy said and kissed me on the cheek. She was wearing a man's t-shirt.

"Stacy, I know it's none of my business, but I don't like that you spent the night with Cody. Especially on my boat."

"I'm the same age as Kailey. She stayed on your, or I should say, *her* boat, with you."

"That was different," I said, and then realized how wrong I was.

35

"You know what was different?" she said.

"What?"

"You were there with her. Cody left last night when you went to bed."

"He did?"

"Yep. I decided to sleep in his bed because Barbie had company at our place last night."

"Where did he go?"

"He just said he had some things to take care of and he would return in the morning."

"Thanks, Stacy. Sorry for the lecture."

"That's okay. I know what it looked like."

"Okay, he's all yours," I said referring to Hank.

"See ya," she said.

I went back to the boat and changed clothes. I was going to go check the local all-night bars for Cody. Later today, I would be with him at the opening ceremonies for the author convention and I wanted him sober.

I debated whether to run or drive. I decided to drive since I might have to hall him home with me.

I drove around the perimeter of the island and checked the few bars there and then worked my way into the inner circle and toward old town.

Betty's Bakery caught my eye as I passed it. In my opinion, she made the best chocolate covered honey buns in all the world. I couldn't resist.

Lucky for me I enjoyed exercise; because this is one vice, I have never been able to kick.

"Good morning, Betty," I greeted as I entered.

"Morning, Cam. The usual?"

"Of course. Make it an even dozen. I have the car today."

"I hope you have some company to help you with these. Sometimes I feel like a bartender. I know when to cut you off."

"I do have company. I left two very lovely girls asleep in bed this morning."

"Um Huh," she said. "Diane and who."

"Stacy," I confessed.

"Cam, you need a woman. You've been runnin' around town with your sorry head hanging down ever since Kailey moved to Colorado."

She was right, but I loved Kailey. I haven't seen her for two months. We were going to fly back and forth to stay together, but the gap kept getting longer between visits.

"I have plenty of women, Betty," I said.

"Um Huh."

I took my box of rolls and got back in the car. Now I wasn't hungry anymore. Betty hit a nerve. I do need a woman.

I looked into the box of rolls and picked a big one. I sat there in the parking lot and ate it. I heard a knocking on my window. It was Betty.

"Here ya go," she said handing me a carton of milk. "Drown your sorrows in this."

"Thanks, Betty," I said reaching for the milk.

"I'm sorry for the lecture, Cam."

"Not at all, Betty. You're right. It's time to move on."

"Good," she said.

"You ever think about being a bartender?"

"And put up with this all the time? No thanks."

She returned to her shop and I finished my milk and roll. I felt better now.

As I was debating if I should eat another, I heard sirens in the distance. First one, then a few more. That was never a good sign.

I started the car and drove in the general direction of the sirens. They seemed to be grouped around White Street Pier.

I parked down the street and walked to the pier. A crowd was already forming and the perimeter was being guarded once again by Officer Mike Horton.

"Hey, Mike," I said. "What now?"

"Guy hanging from the end of the pier," he said nonchalantly.

"May I?"

Mike lifted the tape and allowed me in. I walked to the end of the pier where Leland and three other officers were gathered.

"Another good morning, Cam," Leland said.

"Someone's keeping you busy. Is this the same MO?"

"No, nothing like the others. By the way, the report came back this morning. The hearts were switched. Which means the killer had to visit one of the sights twice without being detected."

"Yes, I read about that last night," I said. "It was all in his book."

"Mind if I borrow that book?"

"Not at all, but don't read it before bedtime."

"I'll need Cody to come to the station today."

"I'll let him know. What is this one about?"

"Looks like someone sent a message to a lover. The guy was hanging upside-down at the end of the pier. He had lipstick on and his, uh, privates were carved up."

"Sounds personal."

"Yep, someone was a little pissed at this guy."

"You have a name?"

"Jerold Tate is what his license says. He's from Houston, Texas."

I thought about that for a moment. We thought we knew the names of the last victims from their license, but we were wrong.

"Did you get an ID of the other two yet?"

"No, we're working on it."

"Any cameras catch this one?" I asked looking around.

"I don't think so. There was only one camera on the pier and someone stole it last night."

"Does it look as if it took place here or was the body moved to this point?"

"We didn't see any drag marks. There is an abandoned fishing pole over here," he said pointing to the other side of the dock. "I think maybe the guy was fishing when someone surprised him."

I took a final look around and told Leland I would have Cody at the station sometime today.

Now I needed to find him.

Chapter 7

When I pulled into my parking lot, I saw a yellow Mustang leaving. The driver was a brunette and quite pretty.

As I stepped onto the boat, I saw Cody sitting at the table. He looked as if he'd had a hard night.

"Back from the hunt," I said.

"Ah, Cam my man," he slurred.

He was drunk again. His white collar had lipstick smeared on it.

"What time do you want to be at the convention?" I said, dismissing the fact that he needed to sober up a bit first.

He looked at his watch. "About one-thirty," he said.

"Okay. Go get in the shower and I'll make some coffee. Chief Leland wants to see you at the station before we go to the soiree."

"Great," he said sarcastically.

"Where were you last night, if you don't mind me asking?"

"I was out with some friends."

"Well, I think you need to slow down a bit. It seems every time you go out you drink all night."

"Not my fault," he said. "I hang with the wrong crowd and really, I don't drink that much."

"Oh, I see. I'll make the coffee," I said and went inside.

When Cody entered the living area an hour later, he was clean and dressed and seemed sober.

He poured some coffee. "Thanks, Cam," he said.

"Feel better?"

"I felt pretty good before," he said.

"You look better though. That should count for something."

"It does. Thank you for watching over me."

"I can't keep doing that, Cody. Do you think maybe you need some help?"

"I do, that's for sure. But not the kind you think."

"Well, I'm here for now. If you want help I'll get you some," I said.

"Thanks."

I gave him one of my donuts. They have helped me sober-up a few times. He devoured it.

"Damn, that was good."

"They're the best in the whole world," I said.

"I believe it."

"Are you ready?"

"Yeah let's get it over with," he said.

I picked the book up off the table and took it along.

"Leland wants to read it," I said.

"Then he should buy one."

"Don't push it."

We sat at the chief's desk. Cody explained the book to him and how the real murders seemed to follow it to a T.

"In the end, it was the author's girlfriend killing everyone so his book would be a best seller," Cody said.

"Do you have a girlfriend here on the island?" the Chief asked.

"If I did, it wouldn't be very noble of me to turn her in."

The chief stared at Cody.

"Okay," he said. "I don't have one."

"Can you think of any reason someone would use your book like this?"

"Between you and me chief, there's some real nut-jobs out there."

The chief sat back in his chair. "Will you please try to think about it for us? You seem to know more about it than anyone."

"Believe me, chief. I haven't thought about much else since it happened."

"Anything new on the other case yet?" I asked the chief.

"No. All we have is his ID. We're trying to find his next of kin now."

Cody perked up. "Another murder?"

"Sometime last night. Down on the pier," Leland said.

"Same MO?"

"No, this was quite different," he said.

"Okay, chief," I said standing, "We have a party to go to. If we come up with something there, we'll let you know."

Just as we were leaving a sergeant stuck his head in the door and said, "Chief, we can't find a Jerold Tate in Houston."

"Okay, I'll be with you in a minute," he said a little perturbed.

"Jerold Tate, from Houston, Texas?" Cody said.

"Yes," Leland said. "Why?"

Cody hung his head for a minute.

"Lipstick, carved-up a little?"

"Don't tell me," Leland said.

"Yep. Right out of, 'Claiming Revenge'," Cody said. "Another Colt Grey novel. Book two in my series."

Chapter 8

We sat back down at the chief's desk.

"Give me everything you know about the murder," the chief said. "I suppose the girlfriend did it again."

"No, this time it was actually done by the girlfriend's mother."

"If it weren't for the fact that you were staying with Cam, I'd be looking at you for these murders," the chief said.

"Why would I murder these people?"

"Like you said in your book. To make it a bestseller," Leland said.

Cody sat quietly. "It wasn't me," he said softly.

I thought about Cody being out all night and seeing lipstick on his collar this morning. He could have done it. I don't believe he did, but he could have. I didn't say anything to the chief about him not coming home last night.

"My book is a bestseller anyway," Cody said. "Trading Hearts, is the first in the series, Claiming Revenge was the second."

"What about one of your fellow authors who's here for the convention?"

"I don't know what they would have to gain," Cody said.

We finished our discussion about the details of the book and left, telling Leland we would be in touch.

We arrived at the Caribbean Palm, at one-thirty. The throng of authors and friends had already begun to grow. It seemed every one of them knew Cody and all bade for his attention.

We mingled with the gathering of authors and fans for a few minutes until I saw my opportunity to excuse myself. I went to the bar and ordered a drink.

Stepping aside so others could get to the outside bar, I bumped into a very lovely young lady.

She was around five-foot-eight, athletic with very short brown hair that spiked in different directions and beautiful green eyes.

"Excuse me," I said. "Are you okay?"

She smiled. "No problem. I was crowding you," she said with a charming accent.

"Would you like a drink?" I offered.

"Don't mind if I do. Wild Turkey, please."

My heart skipped a beat. Now if she asks for a chocolate honey bun, I'll propose.

I handed her a drink and said, "I'm Cam Derringer."

"I'm Emily Chloros."

"Nice to meet you, Emily. Greek?"

"Yes," she said.

"Are you an author?"

"No, not yet. I came with my girlfriend Olivia."

She searched the crowd. "Right over there," she said pointing to a young and sexy woman standing near Cody.

She was the woman I saw driving away from the dock early this morning in the Mustang.

Now, don't get me wrong. Cody's not a bad looking guy by any means, but he has let himself slip a little over the years. This girl, who seemed to want his attention, is a ten on anyone's scale.

I guess there's something to be said about being a rich celebrity.

"Isn't Cody Paxton a friend of yours?" Emily said her tone hinting disgust.

"Yes, he is. We were college buddies," I said.

"I thought I saw the two of you come in together."

Some of the green disappeared from her eyes.

"I take it you're not particularly fond of Cody," I said.

"Oh, he's okay. It's Olivia. She's star struck and married."

"I see. Are you married?"

She looked up at me again. The shine in her green eyes returning. She smiled.

"No, I'm not. Are you?"

"No, I'm not."

She held up her glass and I clinked mine to it. We laughed.

"Are you hungry?" I asked.

"Maybe some hors-d'oeuvres," she said.

We walked to the long banquet tables that were set up on the lawn. Their white tablecloths gently waved in the breeze. We filled our plates with shrimp, chicken wings, and assorted veggies.

We found a couple of empty chairs under a palm tree and took advantage of the shade.

"Are you from Key West?" she asked.

"I am. Born and raised."

"Divorced?"

"Widowed," I said.

"Sorry."

"Thank you."

We ate a few bites.

"Where are you from?" I said.

"New York City," she said.

"I love it there. But I love it here more," I said.

"You have to give it a chance," she said.

"I did for a year, but my circumstances weren't exactly ideal."

"That's too bad," she said. "I hope you weren't mugged."

"Well, yes I was, but that was the easy part. They only stole my chocolate honey bun."

She laughed, "I've got to hear some of your stories sometime."

"How about supper tonight? I grill a mean steak."

"Well, Mister Derringer, you're on."

At that moment, we were joined by Olivia and Cody.

"Hello, Emily," Cody said.

"Cody," she said.

"Cam, I'd like you to meet Olivia Harding," Cody said.

I stood and took her hand in mine and held it lightly. "Nice to meet you, Olivia."

"And you," she said but not releasing my hand.

"Emily and I were just grazing on the hors-d'oeuvres," I said. "Care to join us?"

Olivia released my hand slowly, sliding her fingers down mine.

Her touch was very sensual. I glanced at Emily. She had caught Olivia's flirtatious gesture and blushed, though I think it was from a little anger.

"Yeah, that sounds good," Cody said and placed his hand on Olivia's back. "Come on Olivia, we'll get some drinks too."

He guided her toward the bar.

"How married is Olivia?" I said.

"Not very, it seems. She's been with him every night since we arrived."

"How long has that been?"

"Five nights now," she said.

That surprised me. I thought Cody arrived two days ago.

"Have they known each other long?"

"A few months I believe. She and Tim, that's her husband, haven't been getting along for close to a year now."

"Where have they been staying at night?"

"I don't know. They weren't in our room and they weren't in his room either. Her husband called me at two-thirty in the morning, so I went to Cody's room to let her know but no one was there."

"Cody has a room here?"

"Yes."

My mind instantly went back to the three murders and the time frame. I must have had my suspicions for my mind to go to it that quickly. They could have had time enough to commit them.

"What's Tim Harding like?" I asked.

"Seems okay on the phone, but I've never met him," she said.

Chapter 9

The intimate little dinner I had hoped for with Emily turned into a party of six. Emily and Olivia arrived around five-forty-five followed by Jack and Diane. I would have to try to be alone with her again another time and be a little more discreet about it.

I had stopped at the butcher shop on the way home and bought more steaks. The truth is I loved having friends together. When they're not around I miss them. When they are around, I feel fulfilled. As long as they know when to go home, that is.

We watched the sunset, then the stars appear and then the moon rise. Now I was wishing for some time alone with Emily. That wasn't going to happen.

Cody was getting a little intoxicated, as was Olivia. They went inside to get more ice and reappeared ten minutes later, half-naked. I tried to divert my eyes from Olivia, but I couldn't.

To this point, it had been a sedate, comfortable evening, but I've seen a few naked parties on this boat. I knew what was to follow.

"We're going for a swim," Cody said. "Anyone want to join us?"

Olivia took my hand and pulled me to my feet. "Come on," she said.

"I think I'll pass this time," I said.

Emily rose and stood beside me. "Olivia, one man at a time," she said. "This one's mine."

She hooked her arm in mine and led me inside.

We fixed another drink and went to the side patio where the hot tub was located.

"Nice," she said. "Did you hit the lottery?"

"Something like that," I said.

"Shall we?" she said softly looking at the hot tub.

"We shall."

We did.

The night was muggy as usual but there was a slight breeze helping to keep the mosquitos away.

Emily was not shy about dropping her dress onto the chair and waiting for me to remove my clothes. She was a beauty. Her mannerism's reminded me of Kailey, though her body was different. Her breasts were not large like Kailey's, but they were perfect. Why was I even comparing her to Kailey? Was I going to do this with every girl I met now?

I removed my clothes under the watchful eyes of Emily. She smiled. "Wow," she said.

I was at least ten years older than Emily, but that didn't seem to bother her. It definitely didn't bother me.

We sat close together with my arm around her. It felt good to hold someone again.

Jack opened the door to our patio and announced he and Diane were leaving.

"Be careful," I said. "You're welcome to stay here."

"Diane has an early morning," Jack said. "Cody and Olivia have gone swimming off the platform on the fantail. Their clothes will lead the way if you need to find them."

"Thanks for the warning."

"Nice to meet you, Emily," he said.

"You too, Jack. Maybe I'll see you again before we leave."

"I'm sure you will," Jack said as he closed the door and left.

"Well I guess that leaves us here by ourselves for a while," Emily said snuggling in closer to me.

"I wouldn't get too comfortable if I were you. I'm sure they will find their way here before long."

I leaned toward her and kissed her, she melted into my arms.

We were beginning to get to the point of no return when the door opened once more.

"Cam my man," Cody said. "I'm fixin' drinks. Y'all want one?"

I looked at Emily. She cocked her head, looked at her empty glass and said, "Sure, why not."

"I'll be right back," he said and left us alone one more time.

"I told you not to get comfy," I said.

"You're right about that. Maybe we can lock the door to your bedroom later."

"I like the way you think."

Olivia opened the door next and took a seat in a chair facing the hot tub. She was naked except for a towel wrapped around her.

"You have room for another one in there?" she said.

"Might as well," Emily said.

Olivia entered the tub, dropping her towel and sat on the other side of me. This took me back a few months to Kailey and Robin, my girlfriend and my ex-girlfriend, joining me in this same tub. We had a fantastic night afterward.

Cody opened the door again with a tray of drinks. Thank god, he had on swimming trunks.

Cody didn't join us in the tub but sat in the chair instead. We talked for about a half-hour until he told Olivia to come along. "It's time to hit the road," he said.

Olivia kissed me on the cheek, while at the same time wrapping her fingers around my half-erect penis.

"Thank you for the meal and drinks and the wonderful night," she said looking me in the eyes and not releasing her grip. Things were starting to grow. She smiled.

"You're quite welcome," I said. "I hope you will come back again sometime."

She began moving her hand up and down. She looked at Emily. "Do you need a ride or do you have one?"

Emily looked at me.

"She has a ride," I said. "I'll make sure she gets home safely."

"Alright," she said releasing me and stood only a foot in front of me. She turned and stepped out of the tub.

"Goodnight Olivia," Emily said. "Goodnight Cody."

"See ya tomorrow for the awards and workshop," Cody said as they left.

Emily smiled at me, "I saw what she was doing. Shall we go to your bedroom?"

Chapter 10

I woke in the middle of the night. I could feel Emily next to me. I rolled back over and slept.

The next morning when I awoke, I was in bed alone. I thought back to the night and smiled.

I pulled on my running shorts and went to the kitchen. I could see Emily sitting on the lanai with a glass of milk. That's when I noticed that my donut box had been moved. I opened the box. Two were missing. I removed one and placed it on a napkin. I poured some milk and joined her on the lanai.

"You thief," I said.

She smiled, "Why, did I steal your heart?"

"No, my donuts."

"Those are the best chocolate honey buns I've ever had," she said. "I couldn't help myself. I had to go back for a second one."

"That's okay," I said. "I know where I can get more."

"Have a seat," she said pulling out the chair next to hers.

I sat down and started in on my roll.

"I thought maybe you left. When I woke, you were gone."

"I couldn't sleep. I sat out here and watched the stars."

"I've done that many times myself."

"Tell me about your adventures in New York," she said.

I did. I told her all about the assassin Bloodshot and how he only wounded his targets until the last one, whom he killed right before I killed him in a shoot-out.

"That must have been terrible," she said.

"It wasn't pleasant, but in the end, none of my friends were killed and the man who was killed, deserved it."

She asked more questions about the assassin and then about any other cases I had worked on.

"You seem to be quite curious about me," I said.

"I am. I've never met anyone like you," she said and put her hand on mine.

"I heard there have been several murders right here in Key West in the last couple of days," she said.

"Yes, there have been, but I can't talk about those."

"Is the guy still on the loose?" she said.

"I don't know much about that," I said trying to get her to drop the subject.

"Are there any rolls left?" she said.

"You mean to tell me you can eat three."

"I could eat the whole box, but I'll have to run a few extra miles today."

"Have at it then. You can run with me later."

She helped herself to another roll and another glass of milk. I wished I had her metabolism. I'd love to eat the whole box myself, but I would pay the price in poundage.

When she finished she said, "I could have those for breakfast every day."

"I actually had some sent to me in New York City while I was there."

"Is that what the mugger stole from you?"

"No, I would have shot him for that. It was just a donut from the bakery across the street from Central Park."

"Will you send *me* one sometime?"

"Yes, I will. Just give me your address before you leave."

"Alright. Well," she said. "I had better get going if I'm going to make it to the award ceremony."

"Last night Cody said you were going to a workshop."

"I'm inspired to write. I thought I would drop in on a few of the classes and pick up some pointers"

"Good luck with it," I said. "I tried once. It's not for me."

Emily went in and retrieved her purse. I dressed and grabbed my keys.

When I returned to the living room, Emily was looking at a picture of Kailey that I keep on the bookshelf.

"Who is this?" she asked.

"That's Kailey. She lives in Aspen."

"She's very pretty."

"Yes, she is."

"Is she your girlfriend?"

I was silent for a bit, then said, "Yes, she is."

"That's okay, Cam. I'm only here for a short time and anytime you don't feel comfortable with me being here, just tell me to leave."

"Thank you for understanding," I said.

On the way to her hotel, I got another call from Chief Leland.

"Good morning, I hope," I said.

"No, it's not. There has been another murder. Can you meet me at the Heritage Trail, off 1?" Leland said somberly.

"I'll be there in fifteen," I said and hung up.

"Another murder?" Emily said.

"Yes, I guess so. I'm going to have to drop you off and leave. Maybe we can go for a run later today."

"Can I go to the murder scene with you?"

"I don't think that would be a good idea."

"Please be careful."

"Don't worry about me; just concentrate on writing a bestseller."

"That's the plan," she said.

After dropping Emily off at the hotel I arrived at the Overseas Heritage Trail just an eighth of a mile off Roosevelt, where it meets Highway 1 at College Road. It was easy to find. The morning was lit by the flashing lights of the city police and the county sheriff cars.

I parked off the highway only barely clearing the traffic. I sat in the car for a moment. I wasn't in a big hurry to see another gruesome murder. I wondered where Cody was last night after he left my boat.

"Morning chief," I said.

"Cam."

"What now?"

"Looks like a twenty-eight-year-old male out for a late-night run. He was decapitated. We haven't found his head yet."

"Postmortem?"

"Let's hope so. Look at this," he said pointing at a blood trail approximately ten feet long. "See how the spray fans out?"

The blood was widespread; not in puddles.

"Yeah," I said.

"I think his head was cut off with a chainsaw. Electric is my guess."

"You have an ID?"

"He had a driver's license in his pocket, Thomas Hillerman."

"Any ideas?"

"How many books are in Cody's series?"

"I was thinking the same thing. Someone is acting out the murders. One at a time. I'll call him and see if this sounds familiar," I said.

"Was he with you last night?"

"Until around nine. Then he and his girlfriend went back to the Caribbean Palm Village. I'm sure she can vouch for him."

"Was he drunk again?"

"I'm not sure. I saw him have a couple. We had supper and drinks on my boat. They went for a swim and then left."

"Anyone else there?"

"Jack and Diane."

"Okay, give him a call. If this is another one of his books, I need to see him again. I also think I need to make a visit to the writer's conference."

Chapter 11

I left the scene and drove to Diane's office. I had a lunch date with her today. She was just finishing up with a patient when I arrived.

"Hi honey," I said. "Hungry?"

"Yes I'm starving," she said. "Where do you want to go eat?"

"How about Shanna Key Irish Pub?"

"Fine by me," she said. "I'm doing the fish and chips."

"I've been thinking about their corned beef sandwich."

We found a seat and ordered.

I yawned.

"Did you have a late night?" Diane asked.

"After you left, Cody and Olivia joined us at the hot tub. Olivia climbed in with us."

"You're such a stud."

"Yeah, I know."

The TV over the bar was on. The news commentator was talking about the late-night murder. They were showing footage of the trail where they found the body.

"What happened there?" Diane asked.

I told her the whole story about the murders and the ties to Cody's books.

"What about this one? Does it match one of his stories?"

"I haven't talked to him yet. He and Olivia left the boat last night and went to the hotel"

"I think you had better talk to him as soon as possible. If this matches, he might know where the head is. Then you need to look into his next book and see what's to come," she said.

Our food came and we busied ourselves eating.

I took a bite and swallowed. "Good stuff," I said.

"Yummy."

"What's your professional take on the case?" I asked. "Why would someone simulate the murders from a series?"

"My first thought is to gain notoriety. But that would mean they would have to get caught unless it was Cody himself."

"I just don't think he would do that," I said.

"Then maybe it's someone who wants us to think Cody's living out his stories. Someone who wants him locked away."

"Maybe someone's framing him. That could be."

"Who else would have something to gain if Cody's books became the center of the biggest news story of the century?" she said.

I thought about that.

"A movie producer, for one," I said.

"Sure, or a cop who wants to solve the case."

"Another writer who wants to write about a lunatic author," I suggested.

We ate some more.

"I'd like for you to be present when I ask Cody about this latest murder," I said.

"You mean you want to pretend I'm just there with you?"

"Yeah, you don't have to act like a shrink or anything."

"Will you argue with me if I say I think he did it?"

"Yeah."

"Okay, I'll do it," she said and ate another fry. "But don't kill the messenger."

"What time do you have to be back to work?"

"I have an appointment at one."

We finished our meals, paid and left. The sun was directly overhead now and the humidity seemed to be over one hundred. The salt air mixed with the steam created a mist that opened the sinuses better than any over the counter nasal spray you could buy.

My head felt clear and my senses sharp.

"I'll follow you to the hotel," Diane said. "I'll have to leave in a half hour."

We arrived at the hotel as a group was getting out of one of the classes. We saw Cody talking to several young women.

"Hi Cody," Diane said.

He hugged Diane and said, "Cam, I didn't expect to see you here today. To what do I owe the pleasure?"

"No pleasure I'm afraid," I said.

He got a serious look on his face. "More trouble?"

"I'm afraid so. Can we talk?"

We went to a bench beneath a tree and took a seat.

"Chief Leland called me again this morning. They found a body on one of our trails. A young man, college-age, he was decapitated. His head is still missing," I said.

Cody thought for a moment, then said, "Tommy Hillerman?"

"Yes," I said. "Where's his head?"

"Chainsaw?"

"Yeah. Where's his head?"

"Do you have a golf course?"

"Yes. Right where we found the body."

"It's buried in the sand trap. Hole eight," he said weakly.

"Another book?" I said.

"Book three," he said. "The Trophy Man."

He looked at me blankly. "What the hell is happening, Cam?"

Diane laid her hand on his. "Can't you come up with a theory, Cody? Does anyone have a reason to copy your books?"

"I can't think of why anyone would do this."

"What about revenge? Have you made anyone mad recently?"

"No one. There's nothing," he said.

"What about Olivia's husband," I said.

"So Emily told you she was married?"

"Yes. I understand she and her husband don't exactly get along. Does he know you're seeing her?"

"I don't think so," he said shaking his head slowly.

"Have you ever met him?"

"No, he doesn't travel with her to the workshops."

"She attends the workshops?"

"Yes, she wants to be a writer."

"Is that how you met her? At a workshop?"

"Yes, in Cleveland. A few months ago."

I thought about that for a minute.

"Where is she from?" I said.

"New York City," he said.

"Like Emily?" I said.

"Yes, they met there. If you're thinking Olivia could have anything to do with this you're wrong. She was with me all night and the other nights too."

"No, I wasn't thinking that. I was thinking of her husband."

"As I said, I don't know him."

"Do you know her address in New York?"

"No, but I could probably get it."

"Try to, without her knowing why. I'd like to check on her husband."

"I'll see what I can do," he said.

"I guess now we need to call Leland and he's going to want to talk to you again. We'll need for you to bring all the books in your series with you."

"I've got them on a thumb drive," he said.

"I've got to go to work, Cam," Diane said.

"I'll walk you to your car," I said.

"I'm going to call Leland," I told Cody. "Get your thumb drive and meet me at the station around two."

"Okay, I'm having lunch with Olivia. I'll be there after that."

I walked Diane to her car.

"What do you think?" I said

"He doesn't show any of the signs of someone who's lying," she said. "I believe him."

"He is a storyteller you know. That's what he does for a living."

"Yeah, but I don't think he's telling one now. It sounds as if you want him to be guilty," she said.

"No, I just don't want there to be any doubt about his innocence. The chief is going to want his head on a platter."

Chapter 12

I called Leland and told him where to look for Tommy's head. I knew that wasn't his real name but for now, that's all we have.

Wesley Sparks walked up to the sand trap on the eighth hole.

"Son of a bitch," he said, "It's buried. Give me my sand wedge."

His caddy handed him the wedge and backed away. Wesley was not a good sand player and if you didn't give him plenty of room he would bury you in the sand with his ball.

"Looks to be about twenty-five yards to the center," Wesley said.

"Yes sir," his caddy said. "That would be my read."

More like forty-five the caddy thought, but he knew Wesley wouldn't get out of the sand anyway.

Wesley stepped into the trap and squared himself with the ball.

That was his first mistake, the caddy thought.

He pulled the club back and took a full swing. On impact, the club broke as it came in contact with something solid.

"Shit," Wesley yelled and grabbed his wrist.

When the sand cloud settled they saw something large roll across the trap. Both men walked to the object and bent down trying to figure out what it was. It was red and caked with sand.

"Is that some kind of an animal?" Wesley said.

The caddy took his foot and rolled it over once. They both turned away and threw up their lunch.

I met Leland at the golf course. There was a commotion in the parking lot when we arrived.

A rather large man in yellow pants and a red shirt was standing on the back of his cart holding court.

Leland and I walked to the edge of the crowd and listened.

"Yeah, I took my sand wedge and lined up my shot. When I came through, the ball took off for the hole and my club broke right in half. Then this head comes flying out of the trap and actually hit the green and backspins right back into the sand. I could tell what it was right away but I thought I'd mess with my caddy a bit. I told him to check it out. I said I thought it was a rat," he said and laughed.

The caddy was standing at the edge of the crowd. "Bull shit," he said under his breath.

"Were you there?" I asked him while flashing my badge.

"Yes, sir. Wesley was scared shitless. He threw up at the edge of the sand trap."

"Would you mind taking us there?"

Leland and I commandeered a golf cart from a groundskeeper. The caddy and course manager took another. We followed them to the eighth green

There were several carts parked around the sand trap. Six men were standing at the edge staring into the trap. When we approached they backed off a little.

"Would you men mind staying back," Leland said. "We don't want to contaminate the crime scene."

They opened a gap for us to walk through. The sand was unraked. Not at all like the rest of the traps. At the front edge of the trap closest to the green, there was a red lump caked with sand. It was a mess but undeniably a human head.

"Anyone see anything?" Leland said knowing they didn't but it was a natural instinct to ask.

"No," one of the men said. "We heard Wesley yelling bloody murder and came to see what happened. He took off like a bat out of hell and we found this. Is that a real head?"

Leland ignored the question and stepped into the sand. He asked if anyone had a glove he could have.

"Here," one of the guys said. "It's an old one I save for rain."

Leland put the glove on his left hand and gingerly moved the head from left to right and back.

"I don't want anyone to leave until I have a chance to talk to you," Leland said.

I stepped closer.

"It looks like the golf club caused a lot of the damage," I said. "But the cut marks around the neck coincide with the ones found on the body. Gruesome."

Where the fuck is Cody?" Leland said.

"He's going to meet you at the station around two," I said. "He has an alibi."

"What about his books?"

"He's bringing them with him. He wants to get to the bottom of this as much as we do."

Leland talked on his radio for a minute and then said, "I'm going to talk to the guys for a few minutes. I'll wait for the forensics team. You go find Cody and bring him to my office. He's not going to leave until we figure something out."

"I'll bring him Chief. But he doesn't know any more than we do."

"He might and just not know it."

Chapter 13

I went back to the boat to shower and change clothes.

I opened the squeaky gate and walked up the dock. I felt something tugging at my shoestring. Looking down I saw I was dragging Hank along with me. He was shaking his head and trying to tear my shoestring from its eyelets.

I stopped and picked him up. He licked me again.

"**Hank!**" a frantic Stacy called.

"He's over here with me," I said as she came out on her lanai.

"Oh my god. How did he even get out?"

"He'll find a way. You better batten down the hatches."

"Thanks for catching him," she said.

"Actually, he caught me."

"You've got company," she said.

"On my boat?"

"Yep. Your old friend Walter and his human, Dave."

"Walter," I said. "It'll be good to see him."

I handed Hank back to Stacy and walked to my boat. As soon as I opened the gate, Walter charged toward me. I bent down and hugged him.

"Hey, ole boy. How you doing?"

He licked me and pushed his weight against me knocking me over and then licked me some more.

"He never does that to me," Dave said.

"That's because he sees you all the time," I said getting back to my feet.

"He misses me and all the action."

Walter saved my life when a female assassin was about to shoot me dead blank. He jumped on her giving me enough time to retrieve my gun. But, in the end, it was Kailey who shot her. I was a little slow.

"What brings you here?" I said to Dave.

"I want a favor from you, Cam. Actually, Walter wants a favor. He wants to know if he can stay here with you for a while. My wife kind of threw me out of the house and I'm gonna move in with Crazy Wanda. She's not allowed pets and Linda said he can't stay there with her either.

Linda is Dave's wife. She never did like Walter much.

"Sure, how long will he be staying?"

"I don't rightly know, Cam. Could be a long time," Dave said scratching his head.

"Dave, are you sober?" I said. There was something different about him.

"Yes, sir. I haven't had a drink for three days. I'm trying to get my head straight so I can figure out how to come out of this divorce and still have my boat and car."

"I see. Well, I'm sorry you're getting divorced. I guess she caught you with Wanda again, huh?"

"Nope, she didn't catch me. Wanda was going out the back door as Linda came in the front. Then Linda told me to sit down. She had something she needed to tell me."

"Sounds serious," I said.

"It was. You remember a few months ago when you were keeping Walter cause me and Wanda was going fishin?"

"Yes."

"Remember Linda was supposed to be with her momma cause she was sick?"

"Yep," I said again.

"Well, she wasn't sick and Linda wasn't with her. Linda was with her boyfriend in Atlanta. She met some guy at Sloppy Joe's and they fell in love."

"I'm sorry Dave."

"I'm not. That's the best news I heard in a long time, 'cause I love Crazy Wanda."

"Well, I guess everything turned out for the best then," I said.

"Everything 'cept Walter. He ain't got nowhere to live."

Walter raised his head and looked at me.

"He can live here," I said.

"Hear that, Walter. I told you ole Cam would take you in."

Walter smiled and laid his head back down on the deck.

My life was about to change a bit.

Dave had a sack with Walters treats and water bowls and another with his toys and leashes.

He went to his car and came back pulling a wagon we keep on the dock for groceries. It had two large bags of dog food and his bed stacked in it.

"This should hold him for a few days," Dave said.

"Thank you for the stock. I'll buy what he needs from now on," I said.

"He likes to ride in the car and he has some kind of quirk about hiding his water bowl," Dave said.

"Yes, I remember that," I said.

"Well," Dave said, "I guess that's about it. His eyes were starting to water.

He hugged Walter and told him he would see him soon. Walter licked him and then lay back down.

"You come to see him anytime you want, Dave," I said.

"Thanks," he said. "See ya guys."

Dave stepped to the gate on my boat and stopped.

"Cam, if I don't come back, you take care of ole Walter, hear."

"I will Dave, but why wouldn't you come back?"

"It's a long story, Cam. I think I might have pissed off the wrong people."

"Tell me about it, Dave. Maybe I can help. That's what I do."

"No, you don't need to get messed up in this shit. Thanks for everything."

"I insist," I said.

"No," Dave said. "I already talked to the police and they told me to watch my back. Ain't nobody can cure what ails me."

Dave left the boat and walked up the dock not turning around for a last look.

Walter raised his eyes and watched Dave. He looked at me then lay his head back down. Home is where you hide your water bowl.

I put the food away. Walter walked behind me and inspected the cabinet where I stashed it.

"It'll be right here when you need it," I told him.

I took my shower and dressed in some Nautica shorts a Bahama Jack t-shirt and flip-flops.

It was one-thirty and I needed to be at the police station at two.

I took the leash off its hook in its new storage place. Walter jumped up, grabbed the other end of the leash and starting a tug of war with me. For an old dog, he could be awful playful at times.

I managed to get the leash away from him and hooked to his collar. We went for a walk down the dock.

"Well, look who's back," Stacy said. "Is he staying for a while?"

"Yes, probably a long while," I said.

Walter wagged his whole body when he heard Stacy's voice. She spent some time brushing him and feeding him treats in the past.

"Just a minute Walter," she said and went back into her boat. She returned with a treat for him. When she handed it to him, he laid it down on the dock and looked at it for a second before picking it up again and devouring it. That's something he always does.

We went to a grassy area, mostly weeds at the edge of the parking lot and Walter did his business. I picked it up with a bag, tied it off and deposited it in the trash.

I took him back to the boat and explained to him that he wasn't going to be able to go with me this time. He gave me a sad look and then walked to his bed and lay down.

"I'll be back soon," I said and left.

Cody was walking into the police station when I pulled into the lot. He saw me and waited.

He was wearing white pleated slacks a pink long sleeve shirt and sandals.

"Hey, Cam," he greeted. "Anything new?"

"We found the head where you said it would be," I told him. "This really makes you look bad."

"Yeah, I can see that. I've been thinking about how the story goes in the books. It's a series. Grey solves all the cases. He's a private eye."

"Yeah, so?" I said.

"Just thinkin', maybe someone wants you to solve the crimes."

"That's a stretch," I said. "But I'll do my best."

"That's the only connection I could think of. If someone wants to write a book about me executing the characters in my book, they have to have a hero too. What better person than you?"

"Let's go inside," I said. "Leland's waiting for us and I don't think he's happy."

"Have a seat," Leland said walking around to the other side of his desk. "Did you bring your books?"

Cody pulled a thumb drive from his shirt pocket and handed it to the chief.

"They're all on there. In order. The first three books, you know what happens already. So far, you don't need to read any further than the prologues. I always kill someone in the first few pages and that's where the murders have come from."

Leland turned the thumb drive over in his hand and looked at it as if it was going to tell him what to expect next.

"Stick it in your laptop," Cody said.

"I know what to do with it," Leland barked back.

"We need to look at the prologue for the fourth book," I said. "Maybe we can beat the murderer to the crime scene."

Leland inserted the drive into his computer and started scrolling.

"Two women are tied together and thrown out of their hotel room," Cody said. "Elizabeth Barrett and Donna West."

Leland gave Cody a disgusting glance.

"Why?" Leland said.

"He's a sicko, a hit man. The women had a price on their head."

"Did they get the guy?"

"Yeah, Colt Grey did."

"Who's Colt Grey?"

"The PI in all my books," Cody said as if Leland should have known that already.

"How can we guard all the hotels and all the women in Key West?" Leland said.

"We can't," I said. "But at least we know where to look."

"Cody, I'd like nothing more than to arrest you for these," Leland said. "Not because I think you committed the crimes, but because you wrote the script for the murderer to follow."

"Chief, that's not my fault. There are over three million murder mystery books on Amazon alone. I can't help it that someone picked mine."

"Don't leave town until I tell you that you can go," Leland said dismissing us.

We stood to leave and I remembered Dave. "Chief," I said, "did Dave Richards call you about some trouble he was having?"

The chief paused then said, "No, I didn't talk to him. Do you know where he is?"

"Yeah, he's staying with his girlfriend, Wanda."

"Wanda who," he asked.

"Don't know," I said shrugging my shoulders. "They just call her Crazy Wanda."

We left the station. Cody said he had a date with Olivia tonight.

"Does it bother you that she's married, Cody?" I said.

"It did when I first found out, but frankly no, it doesn't bother me now. She doesn't even like her husband and vice versa."

"Did you get his address?" I said.

"No. I felt funny asking her. I'll find a way," he said. "Emily said she would like for you to join us tonight"

I thought back to last night and smiled to myself.

"Sure, I have no plans. What are you doing?"

"Bar-hopping. We're going to listen to music, knock a few back," he said.

"Okay, I have to go take care of my new tenant first," I said.

"New tenant?"

"Yeah, I got custody of Walter in a divorce."

"Walter?"

"Yep, an old friend who saved my life one time. You'll like him."

"Does that mean I lost my bed?"

"No, he'll sleep on the floor. He's tough."

"Alright then, I'll see you at the hotel at," Cody looked at his watch, "Let's say five."

"Okay, see you then," I said and left.

Chapter 14

I opened and closed the gate to the dock as quietly as possible. I didn't want Hank to come running out and attack me. I walked toe-heal to be quiet.

When I realized I'd made it past Hank, I felt guilty for ignoring Stacy. She has done a lot for me and we have become good friends. I decided I would get Walter and walk back to her boat and introduce him to Hank.

I opened the gate to my boat and heard voices. Emily and Stacy were sitting on my lanai drinking bourbon. Hank and Walter attacked me.

Walter knocked me back and Hank grabbed my flip-flop. The momentum put me on the deck again, and then both dogs went for my face. I was being licked.

The women laughed but offered no help. They continued their conversation and drank my bourbon.

I fought them off and got to my feet.

"What the hell girls?" I said.

"Hi Cam," Emily said. "Stacy was just telling me how she watched you and Kailey making love in the hammock."

"Oh, she is, huh?"

"I wanna try it," she said.

"I wanna watch," Stacy said.

"I think I need a drink," I said. "Why are you guys partying on my boat?"

"I had to bring Walter back," Stacy said. "I saw him sitting on my patio when I looked out the window. Emily happened to arrive at the same time."

"How'd Walter get out?" I said.

"Beats me. Everything was closed up when we came down here."

I looked at Walter. He smiled.

"We have a date tonight," I said to Emily.

"We do?"

"Yep, Cody invited me to go along with you guys to bar-hop and, in his words, knock a few back. He said it was your idea."

"It was. Stacy, you wanna come with us?" Emily asked.

"No thanks. I have a date too."

Hank ran to Stacy and tried to jump up on her lap. His head hit her knee.

Stacy picked him up and said, "I better get going. I need to get ready."

She kissed me on the cheek and said, "You had better batten down the hatches."

She patted Walter on the head and told Emily they would have to do this again sometime and left.

Emily looked at me. Her mouth slightly turned up on one side.

"What?" I said.

She smiled bigger, reached out with her foot and rocked the hammock.

"Not now," I said. "The mood has to be right."

She suppressed a laugh.

I sat down at the table with her, kissing her as I did.

"That was quite an enjoyable night," I said.

"Very, we'll have to do it again sometime."

"Anytime you're ready," I said.

Emily stood and took my hand, "Let's go inside. It's getting hot out here. Don't you think?"

An hour later we entered the shower together, spent.

"Do you feel up to some music and knocking a few back?" Emily said.

"I'd really just like to go back to bed, but it'll be fun."

"We'll find time to do this again."

She put her arms around me and pressed her body against mine. The water ran over my head and down my back. Our lips came together in a waterfall of lust. I lifted her and pressed her against the wall. She reached down and guided me in once more. The steam from the hot water fogged our vision and we melted into a tangle of passion.

We dressed moving slowly through the routine of, one leg at a time.

"I don't know if I'm going to be able to walk from bar to bar," I said.

"Maybe we can get a table at the first one and sit for a while," Emily said laughing softly.

I hugged her and kissed her again. Her tongue slipped into my mouth. We started to breathe harder until I put my hands on her shoulders and eased her away.

"We gotta go," I said.

"Yeah, we better."

We kissed again. This time more passionately. I couldn't push her away again and we lowered ourselves to the floor.

Ten minutes later, "I'm going to get in the shower again," I said.

"I'll join you."

"No way. You wait here I'll let you know when I'm out."

She laughed, then harder. We both started laughing uncontrollably. Finally catching my breath, I got to my feet and went to the shower.

We met Cody and Olivia at the hotel at five-thirty.

"Sorry we're late," I said. "Walter was being a pain."

"I can't wait to meet this Walter," Cody said.

"You'll like him, Olivia," Emily said. "He's cute."

"Why didn't you bring him along?" Olivia said.

"He might pee on the floor," I said.

"What!" Cody said.

"He's a dog, Cody," I said.

"Oh, that explains a lot."

There was a band playing on the lawn. We decided to listen for a while and have a drink before going into old town. We found a table close to the back, away from the booming beat of the band.

The waitress came to our table, "Hi, Cam. What can I get you guys to drink?"

"Wild Turkey for me," Emily said.

"I'll have the same."

Cody and Olivia had beers.

"Cody's been telling me about the book murders," Olivia said.

I shot him a look.

"I told her not to tell anyone," he said.

"My lips are sealed," Olivia said.

"What murders?" Emily asked.

I shot him another look.

"They won't say anything," Cody said.

I briefly filled Emily in on the happenings of the last few days.

"Please don't say anything to anyone else," I said.

They all promised they wouldn't. That did little to satisfy my anger at Cody.

"Do the police think you did it, Cody?" Olivia said.

"Maybe I did," he said and grinned.

"That's not funny," she said. "I could be sitting here with a serial killer."

"Cody has you for his alibi, Olivia," I said. "The murders were all committed in the middle of the night while you two were occupied."

"Lucky for you," she said to Cody.

"I know. Not only do you give me an alibi but I get to have sex too."

Our drinks arrived and the waitress set them down in front of us and then handed me a note. I looked at it. It was her phone number and name.

"I thought you might have forgotten," she said and left.

Emily looked at the note and smiled. "You didn't call her afterward, did ya?"

"I don't know," I said. "I really don't remember her."

"You must be a busy guy."

"No, it's not like that. I would know if I slept with her. I just really don't remember ever meeting her."

I put the paper in my wallet for later. If I can't remember who she is, I'm going to call her to find out.

We finished our drinks and did the town. It was crowded as usual. There were two cruise ships in port, which always made it hard to find tables at any of the bars on Duval Street. I took them to the back streets where the locals hang out.

Around nine o'clock we called it quits. A taxi took us back to the hotel where I bid them all good night.

"Care to join me on the boat tonight?" I asked Emily.

"I think you wore me out today, but I'll bring donuts for breakfast."

"Sounds good to me," I said.

I told her the name of the bakery. "The taxi driver will know where it is," I said.

We kissed goodnight and I went home.

Chapter 15

Jackie and Marty came out of the late-night Character Development seminar feeling energized. The two girls were writing a novel together and felt as though they finally had a grip on their protagonist, Sarah Heart. She would be a strong-willed but giving young beauty, full of life and a thirst for adventure. She would come from a tragic childhood but overcome all odds and would rule her life.

They were eager to get back to their hotel and bang out the details on their laptops.

Jackie had been ghostwriting for five years and was anxious to see her name at the top of the page. She always had to give the credit of her creations to others.

Marty, on the other hand, was the sometime recipient of Jackie's creations but never thought it fair. When she approached Jackie with the proposal they write together and share the fame, she jumped at the chance.

They took a taxi to Duval Street and had a drink at Irish Kevin's, next door to Sloppy Joes where they tried first but couldn't find a table.

They made plans for their future. It was going to be prosperous. They decided to hit a few more bars before going back to the hotel.

They crossed the street to Durty Harry's, where they were able to find two stools at the bar. They sat and each ordered a shot of tequila from Rick's Shooter Bar.

"To our future," Jackie said holding her glass up for a toast.

"May it be long and prosperous," Marty said.

In unison, they licked the salt from their wrists, shot the tequila and took a bite from their limes.

"Woohoo!" Jackie yelled.

"Another?" a male voice said from beside them.

They turned to see a handsome young man they both recognized from the writer's convention.

"My treat," he said.

"Sure," Jackie said. They were going to enjoy their night on the town.

Three more bars and numerous shots later with their new friend, the girls decided if they were going to make it back to the Caribbean Palm, they had better go now.

"I'll see you girls tomorrow at the convention," he said.

"I hope so," Marty slurred.

In their hotel room, Marty opened a bottle of wine while Jackie prepared a snack tray. They took their celebration to the balcony and toasted. "To adventure," Marty said as they touched their glasses together, spilling some on the floor. They drank.

They heard a knock at the door. Jackie set her glass down, "I'll get it," she said.

Opening the door she smiled, "Come on in, we're still celebrating," she said.

Brandon Farley was getting out of his car in the hotel parking lot when he heard a loud thump and his car rocked. He was only halfway out and the jolt knocked him to the ground. When he got up, he looked at the wreckage of his new Chevy SUV. It was smashed right in the middle of the hood. There were two women tied together with rope lying in the center. Blood was dripping down the side of his car and puddling at his feet.

~***~

It was midnight when my cell phone rang. The sound was muffled but I could tell it was near. Rolling over I discovered Walter in bed with me. The sound was coming from him.

I shook him not wanting to scare him and have him bite me.

"Walter," I whispered.

Nothing. "Walter," I said louder and shook him again.

This time he raised his head and looked at me. The ringing of my cell phone continued.

"Shit Walter, did you eat my phone?"

He rolled over and away from me exposing my phone. He had been lying on it.

"Hello," I said turning it on.

"Cam, we've got another murder," Leland said. "Two women at the Caribbean Palm Village. Can you get here right away?"

"Yeah, sure," I said.

"Bring Cody with you," he said.

"He's not here."

"Where is he?"

"He should be there. He's with his girlfriend at the hotel."

"Get here quick, I want to see him right away. What's his girlfriend's name?"

"Olivia Harding," I said.

When I arrived at the hotel, my dash clock read twelve-thirty-four.

Chief Leland had Olivia's room number and was waiting for me in the parking lot.

"Come on I want to see him now," he said.

I could see the crowd in the parking lot. The police had a perimeter taped off again. It was quiet. The blue flashing light should be accompanied by sirens and men yelling, but there was no sound coming from the crime scene. It was as if they were already at the funeral.

I stood back while the police deputy knocked at Olivia's door.

No answer. He knocked once more and identified himself.

Still no answer.

"Cam?" I heard Olivia's voice call from down the hall.

I turned to see her and Emily standing at Emily's door in their nightgowns.

"What's wrong?" Olivia said.

"Where's Cody?" I asked.

"He's in there," she said.

"Wait a minute," Olivia said. "I'll grab my key."

She disappeared back into Emily's room and reappeared with the keys.

As she approached me, she asked again, "What's wrong? Is Cody okay?"

"He's fine Olivia. We just need to talk to him," Leland said.

Leland took the key from Olivia and unlocked the door. We stood back as he eased the door open. The deputy identified himself again.

"Cody, are you in there?" The deputy said. "It's the police were coming in."

We entered the room. Cody was lying on the bed fully dressed, arms splayed in a full T-position. An empty bottle was lying on the floor next to the bed.

I asked Olivia why she was in Emily's room instead of here with Cody.

"He was drinking a little too much," she said. "He does that on occasion. Usually, I fall asleep and sleep right through the night but tonight he was getting a little intense."

"Intense?" I said.

"Verbal," she said. "He would never get physically violent."

"So you went to Emily's to sleep?"

"Yes, I've been waking exhausted lately. I just feel like I need some rest."

Cody hadn't moved since we entered. He was snoring slightly.

"How much did he drink?"

"Well, he drank while we were out tonight and then it looks like he finished that," she said pointing at the bottle on the floor."

"Was he passed out when you left?"

"No, he actually seemed fine except for the anger. Verbally again, not physically."

"What was he angry about?" I asked.

"The murders. He said they were sloppy. In his books, they were always done in a meticulous manner, neat and clean."

"What time did you go to Emily's?"

"Around ten," she said. "Not long after we got back."

"Did Cody stay in his room after you left?"

"As far as I know he did. We didn't hear him leave."

"Let's see if we can wake him up," Leland said.

We each took an arm and pulled him upright. He stopped snoring and his eyes fluttered.

"Hey Cody, you in there?" I said.

His eyes fluttered again. This time they opened. He looked around the room and finally settled his gaze on me. He smiled.

"Cam, my man. Whatcha' doing here?"

"Cody, how ya feeling?" Leland said.

Cody turned his stare to Leland. He took a deep breath and said, "What's going on? Why's everyone in my room?"

He was starting to come out of his trance. I retrieved a bottle of water from his side table, removed the cap and helped him drink a few swallows.

"Feeling better?" I asked.

"I was feeling just fine before you woke me up. What's going on?"

"Where were you around eleven tonight?" Leland said.

"Right here in my bed. I went to bed about ten-thirty," Cody said.

"You didn't leave the room?"

"No. I was exhausted. I remember having a drink and then just going to bed. What's going on?"

"There was another double murder tonight," I said. "Two women tied together and thrown out of their hotel window."

Cody stared at me for a moment. "And you think I did it."

"No, we just want to eliminate you as a suspect."

"Then just ask Olivia. She was here with me," he said.

"She said she left around ten-thirty to go to Emily's room."

"She was here when I went to bed."

Olivia spoke up from behind us, "No Cody, remember you were ranting and raving so I left. I told you I would see you in the morning."

"No, I don't remember that. I must have had too much to drink. I've been doing that lately," he said rubbing his hand over his face.

No one spoke for a minute. Was Cody telling the truth? Or, at least the truth as he remembers it. Could he be committing these heinous acts and not even know it? I really don't think so. If he was so drunk he wouldn't remember, how could he overpower his victims?

"The women," he said, "Were they Elizabeth and Donna?"

"That's what their ID's said," Leland said, "But this time we were lucky. We know their real names from the hotel registry. Jackie Parker and Marty Will."

Cody's eyes opened wider.

"I know them," he said. "They're here for the convention. They're writers. They even did a little ghostwriting for me."

Leland and I looked at each other.

"Are you thinking what I'm thinking?" I said.

"Are you thinking that maybe all the victims are here for the convention?"

"Possibly."

"We haven't ID'd any of the others yet. Maybe someone from the writer's convention should come down and take a look at 'um," Leland said.

"I'll do it," Cody said. "This is all my fault anyway."

"None of this is your fault, Cody," Olivia said. "You didn't do any of this."

"If you wouldn't mind, Cody. It would be a great help," Leland said.

"Sure, why not," Cody said.

"What if I bring him down to the morgue around ten this morning?" I said.

"I'll meet you there," Leland said.

Chapter 16

We let Cody go back to sleep. I didn't think he would be able to after this, but he was asleep before we closed the door.

Olivia said she was going back to their room and get some rest.

"Tell Emily I'll see her tomorrow for lunch if she's free," I said.

"Sounds good," Olivia said. "Is Cody going to be okay?"

"I don't know. I hope so, but there's a lot of unanswered questions."

I bid her goodnight.

Leland and I went to Jackie's room. There were two uniformed officers guarding the room, one in the hallway and one inside.

When we entered the room, the awareness of violence was in the air. What had happened here only an hour ago, left a silent plea for justice. Two vibrant young women were brutally assaulted by an unknown aggressor, unknown to us anyway. There was no sign of forced entry. The door was unlocked. The girls probably knew their attacker. More than likely, they invited him, her, or them into the room.

The sliding door to the balcony from where they were thrown still stood open. The table in the corner held two half-empty wine glasses. One of the women had a sweater folded over the railing. No doubt from the coolness of the room and then removed when she sat on the balcony.

We searched the room but found no sign of a third person. If it was someone they knew, then the assailant might very well be a fellow author here for the convention.

The CSI team arrived. We told them we didn't touch anything and we left them to it.

"I'm going back home," I said. "I'll see you around ten."

"You know Cam, Cody's the only one we have for this. Sooner or later we're going to have to make a decision whether to charge him or not," Leland said. "If we lock him up and the murders stop, it's going to look even worse."

"Yeah, but if they continue…"

We both stood silent for a few seconds, thinking.

"Well, thanks for coming down here," Leland said. "See you at ten."

Walter was standing at the end of the dock when I returned. When he saw my car, he started wagging his tail.

"How'd you get out here, Walter?" I said and patted him on the head.

He walked beside me back up to the boat. I paused at the railing. Walter being outside gave me a sense of insecurity. Did someone let him out? Would he be barking if someone were here? I looked at him. No expression.

"How did you get out?" I said.

He walked to the door, stopped and stared at it. I followed as if he was going to show me something. He just stood there. I opened the door and he walked in. Once inside he just looked at me. He walked back to the door and repeated his ritual. I opened the door and he walked out.

"What the hell, Walter," I said.

"He's trying to tell you that's how he got out. Someone opened the door and let him out."

I turned around startled.

Kailey was standing in my living room. She was as beautiful as ever.

I went to her and hugged her. We kissed.

"What are you doing here?" I said.

"I came to see my number one man," she said. "And it's a good thing I did, 'cause he seems to have a new girl."

I didn't know what to say. I didn't want to hurt Kailey. She has been going to therapy in Aspen, Colorado for the last six months. She had somewhat of an obsession for protecting me. I loved her but I knew I had to let her go in order for her to get better.

"I don't really have anyone I'm serious about but you," I said.

"It's alright, Cam. The therapy has been working wonders on me. I can manage my anger and I don't feel the need to kill everyone who tries to harm you, though I probably would," and she laughed.

"When did you get here?"

"A few nights ago," she said.

"Why didn't you come to see me then?"

"I did, but when you came in you had Emily with you."

"You were here?"

"How do you think Walter got out that time? I let him out to give you a heads up someone was here, but I think you believed Walter could get out on his own."

"I did."

"How long do I have to stand here before you take my clothes off and lead me to the bedroom?"

"Not another second," I said.

We made love until the sun came up.

After a couple of hours of sleep, my alarm went off. I eased out of bed so as not to wake Kailey. I can't believe she's here. My heart was still full of her.

I got in the shower and tried to clear my head. The shower door opened and Kailey stepped in.

"You looked like you had so much fun in here the other night, I thought I'd try it," she said.

"You were here then?"

"Um huh."

"Kailey…"

She put her finger to my lips and said, "Don't say anything."

She wrapped herself around me, holding me tenderly and then savagely. I don't think I've ever experienced such an animalistic lovemaking session. At one point, I felt her teeth sink into my shoulder. I gently returned the gesture until we both exploded into a tangle of limbs and slid to the floor. The water still running washed over us only adding to the tingling nerve ends that were pricking me like a million tiny needles.

Breathing heavily she lay her head on my chest and we faded in and out of blissfulness for the next fifteen minutes silently.

Finally and reluctantly I said, "I have to go. I'm taking Cody to the morgue to ID the victims."

"Yeah, I know," she said and snuggled in even closer.

"You do?"

"Be careful, Cam. All isn't as it seems."

"What do ya mean?"

"The other morning when you woke and Emily was on the patio eating your rolls, she had only just returned. She was gone all night."

"But at one point in the middle of the night I felt her lying beside me," I said.

"That was me," she whispered.

Chapter 17

I kissed Kailey goodbye, "I'll be back this afternoon," I said.

"Be careful, Cam. I love you."

I picked Cody up at the hotel and we drove to the Monroe County Medical Examiner's office in Marathon Key. The drive took us an hour in heavy traffic.

The Medical Examiner, Jerry Devers who I have met too many times, took us into the examination room.

"How do you want to do this?" he said.

"Why don't we start with the first girl and work our way through to the present time," I said. "That okay, Cody?"

"Yeah, I guess," he said sounding a little reluctant.

The Examiner slid open a drawer to reveal a body covered with a white sheet.

He placed his hand on the sheet and looking at Cody, said, "Are you ready?"

He nodded his head.

"The name we have for her is, Tammy Decker from Sebree, Kentucky," Jerry said and exposed only the head and shoulders of the girl's body.

Cody studied her face and then looked away.

"Do you know her?" I asked.

"Yeah," he said. "I met her once a few months ago at a workshop in Chicago. Her name is Karen Dauby. She's my editor. We only work together over the internet."

"Do you know where she lives?"

"Paris, Illinois, I think," he said.

Jerry covered the body up again and slid the drawer back into the wall.

"I'll want to get all the information you have on her when we're finished here," Jerry said.

Cody nodded his head.

We stepped down to the next drawer and repeated the process.

"This is Tony Decker, from Nashville," Jerry said.

Cody examined the body once again.

"Well?"

"I think I know him," Cody said. "I've only seen a picture though. He looks like Allen Parcel from Nashville. He's a voice producer. He does my audio books."

We moved down one more drawer. I didn't like the way this was going. So far, Cody knew the victims and had work ties with them.

"This is Jerold Tate," Jerry said.

"Where's he from?" Cody said.

"Houston, Texas."

Cody paused a moment then said, "So is my producer."

The examiner revealed the body and stood back for Cody to see.

"Jesus," Cody said. "That's him, Rick Johnston."

Cody's shoulders sagged and he put his hand to his forehead.

"Do you want a break, Cody?" I said.

He took a deep breath and let it out. He shook his head, no.

"One more," Jerry said.

"Who is it and where is he from?" Cody asked.

"His name is Tommy Hillerman," Jerry said.

"Yeah," Cody said in a slight daze. "The one with no head."

"This isn't going to be pretty," Jerry said. "We did the best we could to put him back together."

"And he's from?" Cody said.

"Phoenix."

Cody thought for a moment.

"I don't know anyone from Phoenix," he said.

The Examiner slowly pulled back the sheet again.

Cody stepped back. The head looked just like what it was. Sewn-on, with a bandage loosely covering the stitches. The head was cocked back at an unnatural angle as if it were about to fall off.

"Maybe," Cody said and pulled his cell phone from his pocket.

He pulled up a website and tapped on the picture of its host.

"This could be him," Cody said. "Joseph Levi. He does my cover designs."

Jerry took the phone and enlarged the picture.

"That's him," he said.

We left the room and waited for Jerry in the hallway.

"What do *you* make of it, Cody?" I asked.

"All six of them worked with me on my series. The same series that got them killed. I'm the only common denominator here. They're going to try to blame this on me," he said with a little panic in his voice.

"You have alibis, Cody. I don't think you'll be a suspect."

But I was thinking about how the girls said they left him alone. I wondered if they did on any of the other occasions.

Cody filled out a report on each victim. Their contact information and how he knew them. We left them with Jerry who forwarded a copy to Leland.

We drove back to the hotel. I walked with Cody to his room hoping to see Emily. She wasn't in her room or Cody's.

"They probably went to lunch," Cody said. "They're inseparable most of the time."

"Tell Emily I'll call her later today. I've something important to tell her."

"Will do. Would you like to join me for a late lunch? They have a good one set up in the banquet room."

"Not today," I said. "Cody, I was thinking, wouldn't it be better for you if you stayed with me on the boat? That way if anything else happens, you've got a rock-solid alibi."

"I already do," he said.

I told him about the girls saying they left him alone after ten o'clock.

"Yeah, I think they did. I kind of passed out after that. I don't really remember drinking that much, but I guess I did," he said rubbing his hand through his hair.

"Did you see them this morning?"

"Yes, Olivia came in early and climbed into bed with me."

"Does she do that often, or does she usually spend the night with you?"

"No, she usually spends the night with me."

"Okay," I said, "if she was with you on the other nights I don't think they could blame this most recent murder on you. It wouldn't fit."

I left and drove back to the boat. The truth is, I couldn't wait to see Kailey.

I hurried up the dock and onto the boat. When I opened the door and entered, I yelled, "Honey, I'm home."

"How did you know I was here," Emily said.

I was stunned for a few seconds.

"My manly intuition," I said.

I went to Emily and hugged her. I looked over her shoulder for Kailey. Where was she? Was she hiding somewhere on the boat? Come to think of it, Walter wasn't here either.

"Where's Walter?" Emily said.

"I don't know."

"You don't know?"

"He was here when I left."

At that moment, Walter walked into the room. He stopped halfway to us and stretched. Then proceeded to where his water bowl was supposed to be.

He turned and looked at us and then back to the empty spot that usually held his water bowl.

"Where'd you hide it, Walter?" I said.

He slowly turned a circle in the center of the room carefully looking at all the furniture.

"What's wrong with him?" Emily said.

"He's hidden his water bowl and can't remember where."

Emily laughed. Walter looked at her as if he was insulted.

"Sorry," she said.

He walked through an open bedroom door and disappeared. He then reappeared at the door and looked at me.

"I guess he remembered," I said.

I went to the bedroom. Walter stood at the foot of the bed, assumed his pointing stance, aiming at the bed.

I got down on the floor and saw his bowl under the bed in the center.

"How'd you get it all the way in there?" I said.

He ignored me and left the room. I lay on the floor and scooted under the bed until I could reach the bowl.

When I returned to the living area, Emily was rubbing Walter's belly.

"Don't spoil him," I said. "He's an independent soul."

"Except when it comes to retrieving his water, then he needs you."

"That's true, but I think he believes it's a game."

I filled his bowl and set it on the floor. Walter, still on his back, looked at the bowl and then at Emily. It looked like the tummy rub was over so Walter turned over and got up. He drank down half his water and returned from where he came, wherever that was.

"That's one funny dog," Emily said.

"Yes," I said. "What brings you here?"

"You," she said putting her arms around me. "I miss you already."

I wondered if Kailey was listening somewhere on the boat. As if on cue, my cell buzzed. I opened the messenger to see a message from Kailey.

"I'm about to land in Aspen. It was wonderful seeing you again. Let's don't wait so long next time. I love you, Cam and I'm still going to marry you someday.
Tootles, Kailey"

My heart sank. I really wanted to see her again today.

"Kailey?" Emily said after seeing the look on my face.

"Yes," I confessed.

"Did she make it back to Aspen okay?"

"How did you know that?"

"Olivia and I were having lunch today and Kailey appeared at our table. I recognized her from her picture. She really is gorgeous. She joined us for a few minutes, had a drink and said her plane was waiting for her."

I didn't know what to say.

"What did you talk about?" I asked.

"You."

"She didn't threaten you, did she?"

"No, quite the opposite. She said she saw us together and that you talked to her about our relationship. She said she was glad someone was watching over her man."

"That sounds like Kailey," I said.

"Why didn't you tell me she was here? I would have stayed away."

"She surprised me too," I said.

I like Emily, but right now, I didn't feel like making love to her.

"How about an early supper?" I said.

"Sure," she said. "That sounds good to me."

Chapter 18

Chief Leland hung up the desk phone in his office. It was a terrible phone call. It always was when you have to call a mother and tell her that her child has died.

Her mother said she had won a drawing and received a free trip to Key West for the Murder Fest. How unlucky can you be?

He looked at his notes. "I still have five calls to make," he said aloud.

Reluctantly he dialed the next number.

"Hello, is this Mister Parcel?"

"Yes, it is. Can I help you?"

One by one, Leland made his phone calls and one by one, he discovered they all had something in common other than working with Cody.

All of them had won a drawing, which they knew nothing about. Each prize was a trip to Key West for the Murder Fest.

My phone rang while Emily and I were eating at The Captains Table.

"Hello Chief," I said seeing the caller ID.

He filled me in on the coincidence of all the victims winning a trip to their death.

"This sounds very premeditated," I said.

"Yes, it does. And the only other thing we have to go on is Cody's relationship with the victims."

"I think I'll drop by the convention this evening and talk to the committee. I want to find out if there was such a contest."

"Thanks, Cam. I'd rather it be you than me. The uniform sometimes makes people change their story to protect the group."

We hung up.

"What's up now?" Emily said.

"It appears someone made sure all the victims were going to be here in Key West. Did you hear of any contest or raffle drawing for people to win a trip to come to the Fest?"

"No, I didn't know anything about it. There are writing contest where you're reimbursed for your expenses," she said.

"I'd like to see their airline tickets. We might be able to trace them back to the card used to purchase them."

"Why don't you come back to the resort with me and we'll talk to the organization team."

"My thoughts exactly," I said.

We finished our meal and drove to the hotel. There was a large crowd today since it was the last day of the Fest. I saw a board that listed all the sponsors for the Fest. I took a picture of it with my cell phone for later when I could call each and ask about the drawing.

Emily led me to Henry Strait who was overseeing the daily running of the events.

"Hello, my name is Cam Derringer," I said. "I wonder if I could have a few minutes of your time?"

"Cam Derringer? *The* Cam Derringer?" he said excitedly.

"Yes, I guess so," I said a little confused.

"You can have all the time you want," he said.

We walked to a secluded corner where we wouldn't have to yell at one another to be heard.

"May I shake your hand," he said extending his arm.

I shook hands with him.

"Do you know me from somewhere?" I said.

"New York," he answered. "I don't really *know* you from New York. I know *of* you from New York."

"Yes, I was there last year," I said.

"I know, I just finished a novel called, *Bloodgame*". It was based on your adventure there."

"You wrote a story about me killing Bloodshot?"

"I didn't use your name. It was just loosely based on your story though. I was hoping to meet you while I was here."

I thought about that for a moment. I guess there was nothing wrong with him doing that but it felt a little like an invasion of privacy. That would have been a good story for me to write myself. Maybe I still can. I'll name it '*Bloodshot*' and throw in the facts.

"I'll have to read it," I said.

"I'll send you a copy as soon as it's in print."

"Thanks."

"What did you want to talk to me about," he said.

"I'm investigating someone who is at the Fest. It's a domestic case," I lied. "It seems the young lady won a trip here from a drawing of some kind and I was wondering if your organization sponsored it."

He thought for a moment. "No," he said. "I don't know of any drawing for a free trip. But it could have been one of the sponsors."

"Yeah, I thought of that. I'll be talking to them later. I thought I would run it by you first since you seem to be the one in charge."

I figured maybe if I buttered him up, he would be more helpful. He puffed up a little.

"I'll check into it for you," he said. "What is the ladies name?"

I didn't want to give her name out but if there was a contest it might help if they had the right name. I knew none of them knew anything about the murders yet.

"Karen Dauby," I said.

He gave me a funny look.

"Karen Dauby? Didn't you say it was a domestic case?"

Uh-oh, I didn't realize he might know her.

"Yes," I said.

"Karen's not married," he said.

"Her boyfriend is," I said.

He just stared at me. It was making me uncomfortable.

"She was supposed to be in one of my classes this morning but I never heard from her," he said.

"So, you know Karen I take it."

"A little."

He was definitely colder now than he was a few minutes ago. I could tell I was losing him as far as any help went.

"Have you seen her with any men while she was here?" I asked deciding to go for broke.

"Only me," he said. "We had lunch a few days ago and I haven't seen her since."

That's why he was turning cool.

"And I know you're not investigating me," he said. "I'm not married."

"Was that the day we had the bad rainstorm?"

"Yes, earlier that day, before the storm."

"Did she say she had won a contest to come here?"

"She did say her trip was free, but that's as far as we got on the subject."

"Did she say anything about meeting someone else later that night?"

"No."

I think I detected a little anger in his voice.

"Is she in some kind of trouble?" he asked.

"Yes, she could be in a lot of trouble. I really need to know what she's been doing since she arrived in order to help her."

He sighed. "Okay, she was supposed to meet me again last night but she didn't show up. I haven't heard from her. I was a little worried so I went to her B&B. The hotel said she has checked out but no one saw her do it. They said the police were in her room. Is she okay?"

"No, I'm afraid she's not. She's been in an accident."

"An accident?"

What the hell I thought. Maybe it will stir something up. Someone might have loose lips.

"She was murdered two nights ago during the storm after you left her."

Henry turned white.

I watched as he fell back against the wall and then slide to the floor. I've seen some strange reactions to bad news but this was a new one.

Emily said she would go get him some water.

"Are you okay?" I asked.

He didn't answer. For a crime writer, I don't think he ever really considered that these things can happen in real life.

Emily returned with the water and handed it to him. He drank a little and then looked at us as if we just arrived– from Mars.

I put my hand under his arm and gently lifted him to his feet.

"Lean against the wall for a minute," I said.

He did.

"I would like it if you didn't tell anyone about this," I said.

He just shook his head back and forth.

"Now, can you think of anyone you have seen Karen with?"

He looked deep in thought but I don't think his mind was running on all eight cylinders.

"She was with Eric Thompson and Cody Paxton at the welcoming cocktail party," he said.

Emily and I exchanged glances. Cody said he had met her in Chicago a few months ago, but didn't say anything about a few days ago.

"I was with him part of the time during the party until I ran into you," Emily said to me.

"Yes, I remember you," Henry said. "You were with them."

"Do you remember Karen?" I asked Emily.

"No, I'm not sure what she looks like."

"Who's Eric Thompson?"

"He's another mystery writer from Cleveland. No one really likes him much. Kind of a jerk, but Cody's always nice enough to talk to him. I think he feels sorry for him."

"Do you see him around here?" I asked.

Henry looked around the courtyard. "There he is," he said pointing to a man standing alone at the bar.

"Yes, I remember him," Emily said. "He's a little different, but not really that bad."

"Henry, do you happen to know Allen Parcel?"

"I know who he is," he said. "Did he have anything to do with it?"

"No, I don't think so," I said thinking about how Karen ended up with his heart.

I made sure Henry was okay and asked him to keep it to himself again, even though I knew he wouldn't.

"We need to talk to Eric," I said.

Chapter 19

Halfway to where Eric was standing, we ran into Cody and Olivia.

"Hey Cam," Cody said.

Olivia hugged me and then Emily.

"Shall we get a table and have supper?" Cody said.

"I'm afraid Emily and I already ate, but we'll join you for a cocktail."

"Sure, sounds good," he said.

"Girls, would you mind getting us a table. I'd like to talk to Cody for a minute," I said.

"We'll see you at the table," Emily said, kissing me on the cheek. She took Olivia's arm and led her away before she could protest.

"What's up, Cam?"

"That guy over there," I said pointing at Eric.

"Eric?"

"Yeah, how well do you know him?"

"I talk to him occasionally at these events. He's okay. A little rough around the edges."

"Henry Strait said you and Eric were talking to Karen at the welcoming party."

Cody thought for a moment. "Yeah, we were. I forgot about that."

"What did you talk about?"

"Nothing in particular. You know, How ya been, any new books, that kind of stuff."

"Did Eric seem to take any kind of special interest in Karen?"

"Eric takes a special interest in all women," Cody said. "Why?"

"Just covering the bases. I'm trying to find out who she was with the last time anyone saw her."

"That would be Henry, for me. They were huddled together for a while at the party. They looked pretty cozy," Cody said.

"Yeah, another thing," I said, "Leland told me that every victim had won some kind of drawing and received a free ticket for the Fest. You hear of anything like that?"

"No."

"Let's go say hi to Eric," I said.

Eric was around six-foot-two-inches tall and two-hundred pounds. Kind of a handsome guy, well-toned.

"Eric," Cody said, "This is an old school friend of mine, Cam Derringer."

Eric shook my hand and said, "Nice to meet you."

He seemed friendly enough to me.

"Eric," I said. "I'd like to ask you about Karen Dauby."

"That cunt? Whadda ya want to know?" Anger in his voice.

I just changed my opinion of him.

"Did the two of you date or go out for lunch or anything like that?" I asked.

"Not with her," he said. "I wouldn't waste my time."

"Why's that? Is there something wrong with her?"

"I told you, she's a cunt."

"I don't like you talking about her that way," Cody said.

"What are *you* going to do about it?"

With that, Cody swung a roundhouse right and connected his fist with Eric's chin. Eric jerked back a little and then folded to the ground. He was out cold.

"Oh shit Cody," I said. "Why'd you do that?"

"He's a cunt," Cody said.

Henry and three other men came running to Eric. One bent down on his knees and shook him gently. He didn't respond. Next security showed up and separated Cody from the rest of the crowd. One was talking on his radio. I heard him saying something about the police.

Eric was coming around and stood up before we left.

"What the hell?" Eric said holding his jaw.

"I'm sorry Eric," I said. "I don't know what got into him." I was trying to calm the situation.

The police arrived, talked to Henry and escorted Cody off to jail.

I drove to the police station to see if I could get Cody released. After he was booked, I paid his bail and we left together.

"Really Cody?" I said.

He laughed slightly, "I've still got it," he said.

"You know he can press charges and you might be back in jail before the day's over."

"Maybe, but if he had anything to do with Karen's death, he won't."

"And if he didn't?"

"At least we'll know."

I called the girls and told them we would meet them at Schooners. We weren't welcome back at the Fest this year. It was about over anyway, which was not a good thing. The crowd would be leaving in a few days along with all the suspects.

I called Jack on the way to Schooners and gave him all the good news and the details. He said he would go to the Fest and pick up where we left off.

At Schooners, we took a table at the edge of the restaurant where we could watch the people and the boats coming and going. Piña coladas all around.

"Cody, why'd you hit Eric?" Olivia said.

"He wasn't playing nice."

"I told you, you need to learn to check your anger," she said.

"He'll be fine," Cody said and sipped his drink.

My cell rang. It was Leland again.

"I just heard what happened with Cody," he said. "When is he planning to leave the island?"

"Cody," I said. "When are you planning to leave?"

"A couple of days, I guess," he said.

"A couple of days," I said into the phone.

"Tell him not to leave until I say so."

"I'll tell him, but you have to have a reason."

"Okay, assault and battery."

"Oh yeah, I'll tell him."

We finished our drinks. I told the girls I'd like to spend some time with them, but I have to work on this case.

"Maybe I can call you later tonight," I said. "If it's not too late we can find something to do."

"I'm sure we can," Emily whispered.

When I pulled my billfold out to pay the tab, a small piece of paper fell to the ground. I retrieved it and unfolded it. It was the phone number the waitress handed me the other night at the Fest. I checked the name again, Susan Daily. I folded it back and stuck it in my wallet. I made a mental note to call her soon and find out who she was.

Chapter 20

I was starting to worry that Cody was digging himself in deeper with every move he made.

Olivia said he had a bad temper and now after punching Eric, it just supports it.

I still don't think Cody is behind the murders, but he definitely has a big connection. He has scripted each one. I really need to read the prologues in the rest of the series.

Cody stayed back with the girls. He said he and Olivia wanted a little time together.

"Cody," I said, "I need the rest of your books. How many more are in the series?"

"Four more," he said. "I'll be glad to go over 'um with ya."

"Alright," I said. "Maybe when you get home tonight."

"I won't be too late."

I went back to the boat where I was greeted by an anxious Walter. When I opened the door, he ran out and up the dock. He headed straight for the grassy area where he relieved himself.

Poor guy, I must have been gone too long. Maybe that's why he hides his water bowl.

Walter ran back up the dock and in through the open door. I think he likes the air conditioning. I don't blame him a bit.

I called Kailey.

"Hey handsome," she answered.

"Where did my favorite girl run off to?"

"Sorry," she said. "I felt the urge to get back to therapy. I was starting to have visions of cutting Emily up a little."

"I missed you when I returned. I'm thinking of flying to Aspen in a few days. How would that be with you?"

"It's not a good time, Cam. Let me get my head together a little first. Besides you need to be there for Cody."

"I'll give you a week. Then I'm firing up my plane."

"I'm looking forward to it," she said.

"Okay then, goodnight and I love you."

"I love you too."

I fixed a drink and sat on the patio. Cody's book was on the table and I couldn't resist picking up where I had left off.

~***~

Becca Howe decided to leave the Royal Palm and go into town for a little adventure. She had heard of a bar called the Bull where the top floor, The Garden Of Eden, was clothes optional.

She had never done anything like this before but she always wanted too. Now would be the perfect opportunity. She didn't know anyone here, so what the hell. Her husband would never join her in a nude bar or let *her* go.

115

She climbed the steps to the fourth floor and entered an outside bar. A rooftop patio looked a lot like every other bar. That is except over half of the patrons were nude.

She stepped to the bar and ordered a Piña Colada. When the bartender handed it to her, she thanked him and asked where she could leave her clothes.

"Lockers right over there," he said pointing at a row of lockers behind a wall.

"Thanks," she said and walked to the lockers. On the way, she checked out the patrons, both dressed and nude.

She decided it wouldn't matter to her if some were dressed. She wanted to feel the fresh air on her body. It was getting dark so the sun wouldn't be an issue. She just turned forty-six but her body is still good, she thought. My breasts are still firm from aerobics and weightlifting. My legs are sculpted and I don't really have any noticeable wrinkles, unlike everyone else in the room.

She slipped off her shorts and T-shirt and placed them in the locker. She wore nothing beneath either so that was it other than her purse. She had left her tab open so she didn't need her ID. She placed it in with her clothes, closed the locker and removed the key. It was on a wristband, so she stretched it around her arm.

Becca walked around the patio saying, "Hi," to some of the others and took a table near the edge of the patio close to the wall. Before she sat, she walked to the wall and looked over the edge down onto Duval Street. A few people looked up and waved but could only see her from the shoulders up. She smiled and waved back.

She placed her towel, which she picked up from a bin next to the lockers, on her chair and sat.

Perfect, she thought. This is the way she wanted to live her life. She wondered how it would be if she would have never married and had two children. She wouldn't give them up for the world, but…

While she was checking out a well-built man, not to mention well-endowed, she heard a voice to the left.

"Well, well. This is a little embarrassing."

She turned to see a man she knew, *oh shit.* The worst part is he was dressed. She tried to cover herself but there was no way.

"Don't worry about it now," he said. "I watched you walk to the table. Mind if I join you?"

She gave him a twisted smile. "Only if you get naked."

He stared at her, smiled then said, "My pleasure. I'll be right back."

She watched him walking back to her table. *Oh my God!*

"Now may I join you?" he said.

Becca just nodded her head.

"Is this your first time here?" he asked.

She nodded again.

He returned her stare. "Are you okay?"

She shook her head to clear her thoughts. "I'm sorry," she said. "Yes, this is my first time."

"Mine too. I didn't know if I could do it, and then I saw you and…"

"Yeah, it's more fun with a friend. I kind of felt funny sitting here naked by myself."

"Ready for another?" he said holding up his empty glass.

"I guess one more wouldn't hurt."

He stood and went to the bar. He looked as good from behind as he did from the front. He had a few extra pounds on him but shit, *he was hung*. She was starting to have thoughts she shouldn't have.

"Here you go," he said setting her drink down in front of her.

"Thank you, Cody," she said.

He stood for a moment surveying the room. His cock was at her eye level. She couldn't help but stare.

"Have you noticed that we are the youngest people here?"

She looked up at him, "What?"

"We're the youngest people here, well you are anyway."

"Yes, I noticed that," she said.

He chuckled and sat down.

"What brings you here?" he asked.

She stared into his blue eyes and took in his strong jaw and beautiful smile.

"I've always wanted to be free. Don't you think it feels good?" she asked.

"I can't think of anywhere else I'd rather be right now," he said looking into her eyes.

The music was playing and a few couples were slow dancing.

"Dance?" he said taking her hand.

She swallowed hard. "Okay."

Cody pulled her to her feet and they stepped away from the table. He put his arms around her and she did the same laying her head on his chest.

They melted into each other and swayed back and forth. She could feel him starting to get erect.

"Sorry," he said. "Maybe we better move apart a little."

They did but it was too late. She looked down at his hard cock and moved into him again.

"Thanks," he laughed. "That will help hide it."

She started laughing too but soon stopped and hugged him closer concentrating on the hardness rubbing her stomach.

The song ended. "What do we do now?" he said.

"Let's stay close until we get to the table."

They walked together, her in front. When they got to the table, she stood in front of him until he sat down.

"That was a little embarrassing," he said.

"You wanna go somewhere and fuck?" she said.

Now he swallowed hard and nodded.

"I can't leave for a few minutes," he said.

"Let's have another drink," she said. "Maybe things will calm down a little by then. I'll go get them."

He watched her walking to the bar and couldn't believe his luck. He had come here to research a book he was writing. He was going to bring Olivia with him but she wasn't feeling well and said she would rather stay in tonight.

"Here you go," she copied and smiled.

"Well, watching you walk across the room didn't do anything to help this go away," he said.

She reached under the table and put her hand around it. She stroked him a few times and then released her grip.

"Nope, still there," she said and giggled.

They sat and talked for a few minutes while they finished their drinks.

"I think I can go now," he said, "You haven't changed your mind, have you?"

"Not in the least."

They stood by the lockers and dressed.

"No underwear?" he said.

"Don't like it. This feels much better."

Cody took his underwear back off and tossed them into a trash can nearby.

She laughed.

They left and started the long descent to the exit. A man watched them from the bar on the first floor and followed them onto the street.

Chapter 21

I woke early the next morning lying in bed with Walter. Cody's book was resting on my chest. I had almost finished it but fell asleep.

I remembered that Cody hadn't returned yet when I finally went to bed. I had called Emily and begged off going out last night. I still had Kailey on my mind.

I got out of bed and dressed in my running clothes again, as I do every morning with good intentions, not always executed.

I checked Cody's room. His bed was empty.

I put Walter on his leash to take him for a long walk instead of running. Occasionally I would run and he'd gladly keep up without protest. It was probably as good for him as it was for me.

However, when I reached the parking lot I saw Cody's car parked there. I looked inside and saw him lying in the front seat. I knocked on the window. He didn't move so I tried the door. It was unlocked. I shook him and he finally stirred and sat up.

"What the hell?" he said.

"Were you out here all night?" I asked.

"I don't know. I don't remember even driving here," he said looking around trying to figure out how this happened.

"Come on in and I'll fix some breakfast," I said.

I fixed breakfast and fed Walter. He was energized from the walk to the parking lot and back.

"Sorry boy, I'll take you out later for that walk."

He gobbled his food instead of his usual pushing it around the kitchen a few times first.

Cody appeared just as the pancakes were coming off the griddle.

"Yum," he said. "I hope some of those are for me."

"It's your lucky day."

He sat and I placed a stack of cakes in front of him then poured more batter onto the griddle.

"Sorry I was out so late last night," he said. "I ran into a friend and couldn't get away."

"Don't worry about it. I had a nice, peaceful evening here reading."

"Anything good?"

"Your book. I almost finished it."

"Glad to see you're improving your repertoire," he said.

"Now if I could just sleep after reading it. That reminds me, I want to see the rest of your books."

"I'll get them as soon as we finish breakfast."

Another helping of pancakes and he announced he couldn't eat anymore.

Cody's overnight bag was stored in his bedroom. He dug through the bag and pulled out a thumb drive and handed it to me.

"We'll have to use your laptop," he said. "Mine's in my hotel room."

I slid it in and Cody brought up the books.

"Here are the first four books," he said sliding the cursor down the row. "They're the ones the murders have already been acted out in."

"There have to be thirty books here," I said.

"Close," he said, "Thirty-two, but only these eight are in the Colt Grey series."

"Here's the next one," he said pointing to another title.

"Death Lake."

"Is there a murder in the prologue again?" I asked.

"There's a murder in every prologue."

"What happens here?"

"A deserted road outside a small town. A skinny dipping lake. You can figure out the rest," he said.

"What'd he do to him?"

"*She* was staked down with her wrists cut."

"Staked down?"

"I'm afraid so."

"How does Colt catch this guy?"

"Good detective work. He figures out it has to be someone from the town. After scanning their pasts and then their habits, he has a suspect. He sets up a decoy and they get the guy."

"Sounds easy enough," I said.

"There's a lot more to it. That's the short version. The victim didn't die, but she never could ID her attacker. Turns out it was someone she knew."

I had to think about that for a minute. The keys are fairly crowded everywhere, but there are a few back roads.

"The closest small town around here with what could be considered a deserted road is Geiger Key. Boca Chica Road doesn't have much traffic. There's actually a barrier set up to stop the traffic. You have to proceed on foot from there. Boca Chica Beach has a clothes optional area."

"That sounds like the perfect setting, Cam. We should set up a guard there," Cody said.

"I'll call Leland and try to get someone there right away. Meantime, I think I'll go myself and look around," I said.

"I'll go with you," Cody said.

As I opened the door to leave, Walter made his escape again.

He stopped at the gate and looked at us.

"Come on boy," I said in my childlike voice I use to call him.

He turned and ran through the gate and to the car.

"I've seen this before," I said. "It looks like he's going with us."

"That's fine," Cody said. "He's good company."

"Grab my laptop. I want you to read the other prologues to me as I drive."

We headed north on the overseas highway, past Stock Island. The Key West Naval Air Station was on our right. We passed it and drove to Big Coppitt Key where we turned right toward Geiger Key. We followed 491 to Boca Chica Beach.

On the way, Cody read three more very gruesome murders to me.

One murder consisted of a man tied to a post on a target range. Bails of straw were stacked in front of him hiding him from the view of the early morning patrons. The targets were already fastened to the straw. After about two-hundred rounds were fired one of the marksmen went out to check the targets. The guy who had been tied and gagged was shot sixty-four times.

Another man was secretly chained to a semi at a truck stop. His hands were tied behind him and he was gaged. They found parts of him for the next thirty-five miles.

The final murder was the most unnerving. Colt Grey's daughter was kidnapped and tied to a chair in an abandoned house. The house was rigged so when Colt entered to save her, it would set off a volley of small explosions engulfing the house in flames.

Colt is the PI who solves all the crimes. The only person around here that would resemble Colt, is me. Is that what this was leading to? Is someone going to kidnap Diane just to finish off their murder spree?

We arrived at the beach. There were several cars parked on the road at the barrier.

"I guess there are a few nude people out here," I said. "Can you handle that?"

Cody laughed, "It depends," he said.

The sun was hot overhead as we walked out to the beach. Walter insisted on tagging along. There were several people sitting on blankets and a few in beach chairs. They were all nude, and old and mostly men.

We passed them and walked down the road a few hundred yards.

"This would make an easy place to attack someone at night," I said. "But during the day, there're probably people around."

I noticed a small path leading off away from the beach and decided to investigate. After about fifty yards, Walter took off running. When he was out of sight, I heard him barking.

"Walter!" I yelled.

I hoped he hadn't surprised a couple trying to find privacy for some romantic encounter.

I made the turn and saw Walter still barking and looking into a patch of tall weeds about thirty feet off the trail.

I went to him and saw what he was barking at. There in the weeds was a young girl, stripped bare, gaged and staked to the ground. There were trickles of blood on her wrist. She looked as though she was sleeping. Her breath was shallow but evident. She was still alive.

Cody looked at her and shock came over his face.

"Rebecca Taylor," Cody said. "Goes by Becca. She's my proofreader."

Cody slumped to the ground and stared at her. He dropped his head into his hands.

"I'll cut her loose," I said. "Give me your shirt."

I untied her and slipped my shirt on over her head. We used Cody's shirt to make some tourniquets and wrapped them around her wrists. She wasn't able to talk or respond in any way but I thought she had a good chance of surviving. By the time we got her stable enough to carry, we could hear the ambulance coming up 491.

If she makes it, we have a witness.

When the ambulance left, we went to the beach to question the folks that were still hanging around. All but one had dressed when the excitement started. He wasn't a pretty sight. Five-foot-ten or so, two-hundred-fifty if he was a pound and I won't describe the rest.

"Did any of you see anyone come or go on that trail during the night?" I asked.

They all looked at each other and kind of shook their heads in unison.

"What about the young lady? Was she here on the beach before?"

"I've never seen her," the naked man said.

Walter looked at him and moved behind me. He peeked around my legs at him again.

"Was there another car here that you haven't seen before?"

"Not that I noticed," he said.

Great, the only one who will talk to me is the one I'm trying to not look at.

I pulled my cards from my wallet and handed them out.

"Please, give it some thought and if you come up with anything you remember being a little off, call me."

They all said, "Okay," and nodded their heads while looking at my card.

I knew I was finished here. These people probably didn't want anyone to know they were here.

The naked man reached out to shake my hand, "Nice to meet you, Cam. We'll call if we remember anything."

I reluctantly shook his hand.

Chief Leland asked them to stay a few minutes longer while he took some statements. We left.

Chapter 22

We met Leland at the hospital after we dropped Walter off at the boat. We were hoping for a chance to talk to the victim. Her purse was lying beside her with her ID in it. We already knew the ID wouldn't be hers. Cody verified this when I read him the name, Linda Rhodes.

"Yeah, that's her name in the book," Cody said.

We went to the ER and waited. They were working on her, hooking up IV's and propping her up so she wouldn't choke. She was very dehydrated.

The doctor said we could look in on her, but she wouldn't be awake for at least another twenty-four hours.

Standing at the foot of her bed, she looked like a child. She was swollen from the sun and bruised from the fight she must have put up. Her wrists were bandaged but the doctor said the cuts were almost superficial. Someone didn't want her to die too quickly.

"Rebecca Taylor," Cody told Leland. She proofreads my books before I send them to the publisher."

"How old is she?" He asked.

"Forty-five, give or take."

"Do you know where she lives?"

"Fort Myers, Florida with her husband and two children," he said.

We stared at her in silence for a bit. Her family has no idea and now we have to inform them that they almost lost her. Thank God, we arrived when we did.

"In the book," Cody told Leland. "It was the same. She was found before she died."

"You think someone wanted us to find her?" Leland said.

"I would think so," he said. "If they wanted to follow the book."

"Did Linda Rhodes ID the person who abducted her?" Leland asked.

"No, she never saw them."

"I guess Becca never saw her attacker either."

"That would be my guess but you never know."

Leland took down Becca's information from Cody and said he'd call her husband right away.

On the way back to the boat Cody was quiet.

"Is something wrong, Cody?" I asked.

"Yeah Cam, there's a lot wrong," he said.

"What is it."

"Becca," he said. "I was with her last night."

"You were out with Becca?"

"Yeah. We were at the Garden of Eden above the Bull. We kind of got naked and one thing led to another. We decided to go to her place to fool around."

"Jesus, Cody. What happened?"

"I don't know. We were walking through the parking lot and that's the last thing I remember. I woke up in the car this morning still dressed."

"Were you drinking a lot?"

"We had two drinks at the bar. Other than that it was just the drink we had at supper."

"Why were the two of you at that place and where was Olivia?"

"I was researching a book and Olivia said she didn't feel well, so she didn't go."

"You don't remember going to Boca Chica Beach?"

"No, I don't remember anything after we arrived at the hotel."

"Keep this to yourself for now. We'll figure it out," I said.

Cody and I went back to the boat where I left him with Walter while I went back to the hotel.

I found Jack in the lobby. Diane was with him.

"Did you find out anything new?" I asked.

Jack pulled out his notebook and flipped a page over as if he were going to read me the report.

"No," he said.

Diane giggled.

"Don't encourage him," I said to her.

"Eric seemed to be okay," Jack said. "He left right after you did from what Henry told me."

"There's been another incident," I said. "Cody and I found his proofreader staked to the ground at Boca Chica Beach. She was still alive, just like in the book."

"Someone's sick," Diane said.

"Isn't that a nude beach?" Jack said. "What were you and Cody doing there?"

Diane giggled again.

I gave them both, the look.

Emily appeared at my side. She was dressed in a short, thin, low-cut, flowered dress. I kissed her.

"You look marvelous," I said.

"Thank you. That's what I was going for."

"Where's Olivia?"

"I haven't seen her since I woke."

Just then, Olivia said, "Hi guys."

She hugged everyone.

"I see you finally woke," she said to Emily.

"Yes, finally. I've been sleeping a lot lately. I think it's the jet lag."

"You'll get over it about the time you have to go back to New York," Olivia said.

We were making small talk when Eric walked up.

"Where's your friend?" he asked me.

"In a safe place," I said.

"He didn't need to hit me."

"I think he did."

"Why?"

"The girl you were referring to is dead," I said.

"Dead?"

"Yes, she was murdered two nights ago."

"Oh, I'm sorry to hear that. I didn't mean anything by what I said."

"It's a little late for that," I said.

"Who did it?"

"We're not sure, yet. However, we'll find out."

"I hope so," he said. "Tell Cody I'm sorry."

I thought Eric was more than forgiving. I didn't know if I could apologize to someone who knocked me out.

"I'll tell him," I said.

"I hate to leave good company again," I said, "But, I have some questions to ask. I still hope to see you later today," I said to Emily.

"I can't wait around forever," she said and kissed me on the lips very sensually.

"I'll try to make it quick," I said.

"Where's Cody," Olivia asked.

"At the boat. He's not welcome here."

"I think I'll go see him," she said.

"Be gentle with him, he's had a rough day."

"Yes, he spent the evening in a nude bar,' she said.

"It was in the line of duty."

"Yea, right," she said.

~***~

I left there and went to The Bull. I climbed the steps to the fourth floor and approached the bartender.

I showed him my badge and a picture I had of Cody and asked if he saw him there last night.

"Sorry, man. I was off yesterday. Stan was up here. He's down on the second floor today."

"Thanks," I said. "I'll go find him."

I turned and looked at the few people who hang out and I mean that literally. I turned back to the bartender.

"Do any of these people visit on a regular basis?" I asked.

He scanned the crowd. "Yeah, that couple over there," and pointed to a couple in their mid-seventies.

I went to them trying not to look. This was getting old.

"Hi," I said flashing my badge again.

"Are you going to frisk me?" the woman said.

I chuckled, "No ma'am, I'm just looking for a little info."

"Too bad," she said. "You're not here to frisk him are you?" she said pointing to her husband and belly laughing.

"No, I'm not here to frisk anyone."

I held the picture of Cody out and asked them if they might have seen him here last night.

"Look, Fred," the woman said. "It's the guy with the hard on."

Fred took the picture from me and held it close to his face.

"Ha! It sure is. That guy's got a real wonker on em."

"Did you see him leave with anyone?" I asked ignoring the comment.

"Yeah," Fred said. "The most beautiful girl in the room. Next to my Sara of course," and hugged her.

She slapped him on the arm.

"Did they seem to be drunk?"

"Not that we noticed. He wasn't too drunk to get all hard while they were dancing."

I was getting more information than I wanted. I hoped I could get the image out of my mind.

"Was anyone with them?"

"Nope," Sara said. "Just those two but I wish we would have left with em."

I thanked them and left to look for Stan.

I found Stan at the bar downstairs and repeated the questioning.

"Yeah, she had a killer body. Him, a little heavy but you could tell it was recent weight. He looked like he might have had some muscles in there. He was hung like a pony though."

Enough! I gotta get out of here.

"They didn't leave with anyone?"

"Not that I saw. I don't think they wanted anyone else."

I thanked him and left.

Now, my main suspect is Cody. I have to prove he didn't do any of this but he's making it difficult. I was having a hard time convincing *myself* he was innocent, much less everyone else.

Chapter 23

Cody and Olivia were sitting on the lanai when I returned.

"Hi, Cam," Olivia said. "Cody was just telling me how awful the sights were at The Garden of Eden."

"Really?" I said. "He told me the girls were fantastic."

She shot him a look.

"Don't believe him," Cody said. "He's trying to get me in trouble."

I fixed a drink and joined them.

"What are your plans for the day?" I asked them.

"We're just hanging out. Thought we'd go listen to some music," Cody said.

"I want him to take me to the Garden of Eden," she said.

She looked at Cody and he glanced at me. I gave him a subtle shake of the head indicating, no.

"I don't think my stomach could take it again and it's no place for a lady like you," he said.

She just shook her head and took a drink.

"Have you heard any more about the young girl you found this morning?" Olivia asked.

"Nothing yet. They said it might be tomorrow before she could have a visitor."

"I hope she'll be okay," she said.

"They seem to think she'll make a full recovery."

"I wonder where they abducted her from?"

"We don't know, yet."

I excused myself and went to check on Walter. I wanted to get away from Olivia before she asked a question I didn't want to answer. I don't know how much Cody has told her.

A minute later Cody came in.

"Did you find out anything about last night?" he asked.

"Only things about you I didn't want to know," I said. "It seems the two of you put on an unforgettable performance."

"Oh, that," he said. "Couldn't help it. You saw her."

"Yes, I understand. No one saw anyone leave with you."

"Something happened in that parking lot," he said. "Let's go check the cameras there."

"I'll go check the cameras. You stay away from there. Every time you go there something happens."

"Fair enough."

"What time did you arrive at the hotel?"

"Around eleven-thirty, I'd say."

"Okay, I'll check it out. I have a few other things to check on too, so I won't be back till late."

I kissed Olivia goodbye and drove to the Royal Palm. I checked with one of the security personnel when I arrived and he directed me to their main office where the recorders were located.

An aging security guard was perched on the corner of his desk watching The Wheel of Fortune on his TV. He jumped up when I entered and turned off the TV.

"Can I help you?" he said in an official voice that he couldn't really pull off.

I flashed my badge and asked about last night's parking lot cameras.

"Sure," he said "What time?

"Around eleven to twelve," I said.

He was reaching for the remote when I gave him the time. He stopped.

"Let me check something out first," he said.

He picked up a clipboard and flipped a page.

"Yep," he said. "We don't have it."

"You don't have it?" I said.

"No, somehow the power to our cameras was turned off last night around ten-thirty and we didn't get them back up and running until around two a.m."

"So, you have no record of the parking lot between those hours?"

He just looked at me. "Right," he finally said.

Another dead end but the fact that the cameras were killed tells me something happened in that lot.

It was getting dark now, which is what I was waiting for. I drove to the pier where Rick Johnston was mutilated and murdered. Sometimes the same people hang out in the same places every night after dark.

I questioned anyone who happened by. One man remembers two men fishing at the end of the pier in the early evening. One was a little overweight and short, the other was taller and well built. Their fishing hats covered most of their faces, so he couldn't really give a good description. He said he remembered them because he had never seen them before and he's here almost every night.

Rick Johnston fit the description of the shorter man, but Cody didn't fit the other.

"Did you see anyone else, around that time?" I asked.

"A few people here and there. There always is. There was a couple fishing off the side of the pier right over there," he said pointing to a bench. "I think they were more into kissing than fishing."

"Are they regulars?"

"No, I've never seen them either, but we do get a lot of tourists just wanting to enjoy the evening, and maybe catch a fish or two."

"May I ask why you come here every night?"

"Personal reasons," he said.

I let it go.

"Thanks for the info," I said and handed him my card. "If you think of anything else, will you call me?"

"Sure will," he said.

There wasn't much more I could do tonight so I called Emily and she agreed to meet me at the boat.

I arrived first and let Walter out. He was grateful for the break. I noticed his water bowl was missing.

I had expected Cody and Olivia to be there, but they weren't.

I was sitting on the lanai having my first drink when Emily came up the dock with Walter in tow.

"I see you found him," I said.

"He found me."

"Well, either way, I'm glad you're both here," I said standing to kiss her and pat Walter on the head.

Walter licked my hand and went inside.

Emily had a sack in her hand. Without even asking, I knew what it was. I would recognize that sack anywhere.

"I see you're planning to stay for breakfast," I said.

She shook the sack. "Betty's Bakery," she said.

I took the sack in and placed it in the microwave to keep it fresh.

I noticed Walters's water bowl was back in place, where it belonged. I filled it while he watched. I think he was grinning at me. I knew he was messing with me. Weird dog.

When I returned to the lanai, Emily had fixed herself a drink and removed her clothes.

"Join me?" she said.

I took off my clothes and settled in beside her on the chaise longue.

"Nice," I said.

The stars filled the night sky and the three-quarter moon cast shadows on the deck. Though I knew no one could see us, I felt as if we were in perfect sight of the world.

My feelings were usually on point.

Chapter 24

When I woke the next morning, I could tell it was late. The sun was coming in my window. Emily was still lying in bed next to me. I could see the shallow rise and fall of her breasts, so I knew she was still alive.

I made coffee to clear my head, which was foggier than usual. I picked a chocolate roll from the bag and took my treasure to the lanai. Before I made it out the door, I remembered Walter. He usually had me up by now wanting out.

I walked around the first floor but didn't find him anywhere. His water bowl was still neatly tucked into its allotted space.

I opened the door and stepped onto the lanai. He was lying under the patio table. I must have woke him because he stood up quickly and bumped his head. That didn't seem to bother him any. He was more interested in my roll.

"No way, buddy. Chocolate is like poison for a dog," I said.

I don't think he believed me because he never took his eyes off the roll.

"How'd you get out here?"

His answer was a lunge at my roll. I was too quick for him. I stood and opened the door. He went in before me and I closed the door. He turned and looked at me through the glass. He probably felt like a fool.

I took a bite of my roll and set it down on a napkin while I sipped my coffee. Life doesn't get any better than this.

The sliding door opened and Emily walked out. Walter almost knocked her down. He made a quick grab at my roll and took off down the dock with my roll hanging from his mouth.

"**Walter!**" I yelled.

He kept running.

Emily laughed, "Did he just steal your roll?"

"Can you believe it," I said. "That does it; I'm calling Dave to come to get him."

"You'd miss the ole boy if he was gone," she said.

"He has no respect for other people's property."

"Didn't you tell me he saved your life one time?"

"Yeah, but...."

"I'll split my roll with you," Emily said.

"It's just not fair."

"Life can certainly be tough sometimes, but I don't think this is one of those times," she said, teasing me.

"Did you get up last night and let Walter out?" I asked.

"No," she said. "I was out like a light. I don't even remember if we made love or not."

I thought back about last night, "I don't either," I said.

"We must have been really tired by the time we went in."

"I do remember the two of us sitting out here in the nude," I said.

"Yeah, that was nice."

"Cody and Olivia never came back," I said. "I guess she snuck him into the hotel."

"They're wild together."

My cell phone rang. The caller ID said, "Leland."

"This can't be good," I said.

"Good morning, Chief,"

"Another murder," he said. "This morning on Ram Rod Key."

"Firing squad?" I said.

"More or less," Leland said.

"Are you still there?"

"Yeah."

"I'm on my way."

"Okay, you know the old trail by the Cucumber Corporation?"

"Yes."

"Turn in there and I'll meet you."

"Okay."

"Where's Cody?" he asked.

"I don't know," I admitted.

"He wasn't with you last night?"

"No, he was with Olivia."

"See if you can get in touch with him. If you can, bring him with you."

I called Cody but got no answer.

Emily called Olivia. She answered.

"Is Cody there with you?" she asked Olivia.

"No, he went out late after we had our time together. I haven't seen him. I thought he would probably be at Cam's, but if you're there I guess he's not."

"If you see him, have him call Cam," Emily said.

"Is something wrong?"

"Another murder, right out of his book," she said.

"I'm going to go look for 'em," Olivia said. "I know his haunts."

I arrived at Ram Rod Key around nine-thirty. I was met at the top of the road by Leland and Sheriff Rogers. I had met the sheriff a few times. He wasn't a bad guy, but I didn't have much faith in him. He took over for Sheriff Toby Reynolds when he was murdered and fed to the Gators in alligator alley. Toby had taken over for Sheriff Buck when he was killed trying to kill me.

"Some guys stopped at the Big Coppitt Gun Club this morning and bought some ammo," the sheriff said. "They were gonna' pay to use the shooting range, but there was a guy there who told them he had a range set up here," he said pointing down the road, "And they could join him and shoot for free."

"Are they still here?" I asked.

"Yeah, they're over there leaning on that truck," he said and nodded toward three guys next to their truck. "Anyway, after about three boxes of bullets were fired the other guy left. They fired a few more boxes and then went to replace the target. That's when they found the guy tied up behind the straw."

"Do we have an ID on the first guy?"

"Tall, hat pulled down on his head, sunglasses and a beard. One guy swears the beard was fake."

"Heavy or thin?"

"Pudgy. One guy said he thought maybe that was fake too, but the other two say it was real."

"Not much to go on there," I said. "Why didn't they check the guy out a little better?"

"He had liquor and gave them plenty of it," Rogers said. "They didn't ride together and he kept his distance while they were shooting."

Another dead end and Cody was looking good for every murder.

Chapter 25

Olivia went into Cody's room. He was lying on the bed fully dressed. On the table next to the bed was what appeared to be an animal of some kind. It was a fake beard. She picked it up and inspected it, laid it back down on the table and shook Cody. He only groaned and rolled over.

Olivia picked up his phone and checked the volume. It was turned all the way down. She turned it up and checked the caller ID. She and Cam had tried to call him this morning.

"Cody," she said shaking him again. "Come on, wake up."

He rolled over again and opened his eyes. He saw Olivia and smiled.

"Good morning," he said.

"Get up," she said. "I'm going to get you some coffee."

Olivia left the room. Cody sat up on the side of the bed and looked around the room. The last thing he remembered, he was in bed with Olivia in *her* room.

He saw the fake beard on the table and picked it up.

"What the hell?" he said.

His cell rang. The caller ID was blocked.

"Hello," he said.

"I saw you last night," an unfamiliar man's voice said.

"Who is this?"

"I saw you early this morning too, at the shooting range."

"What shooting range?" Cody said confused.

His phone disconnected.

Who the hell was that?

Olivia returned with coffee for her and Cody.

"What's this," he said picking up the beard.

"I don't know. I figured you'd tell me."

"I've never seen it before," he said.

"It was laying there when I came in," Olivia said.

"Why aren't I still in your room?"

"You left last night after we made love."

"I don't remember that."

Olivia hesitated.

"What's wrong?" Cody said.

"There was another murder early this morning," she said.

Cody thought a minute. "Firing range?"

"I don't know, but Emily said it was just like in your book."

Cody looked around the room. His shoes were at the foot of the bed. They were muddy.

Olivia saw him look at them and she looked too.

"How'd you get mud on your shoes?" she asked.

"I don't know."

"You need to call Cam," she said.

When Cody called me and asked me to come to his room, he sounded a bit worried.

I soon realized he had a good reason.

"And you don't remember going out last night?" I asked.

"Not at all," he said.

"You don't know where the beard came from?"

"No."

"Was anyone else with you last night?" I asked Olivia.

"It was just us. We bar hopped earlier, but then we came back here. We made love and Cody said he was going back to his room. We sometimes part ways after we make love. I didn't think anything of it."

I looked at his shoes and then mine. Mine had a small amount of soot on the sides of the soles. Cody's were covered on the sides and bottoms. It looked like the same mud. Mine was picked up at the Cucumber Corporation area, so I surmised Cody's could have been too.

"I got a phone call a while ago too," Cody said. "The guy said he saw me at the shooting range early this morning. I wasn't there."

"You didn't recognize the voice?"

"No, it sounded disguised."

"Keep that to yourself. We'll figure it out. We need for you to come to the morgue again and ID the most recent body. He was shot over forty times."

Cody ID'd the man as Ben Striker. He did the layout and printing for his books.

"I only met him for the first time a few days ago," Cody said. "We did all our communicating over the internet."

Leland got a call while we were standing in the corridor leading to the autopsy room. He listened for a minute and said, "Okay, thanks."

"Cody," he said, "I'm afraid I have to take you in for questioning."

"Why."

"We received a tip that you were spotted at the crime area this morning. We got a warrant to search your room. The mud sample we took from your shoe matched the area where we found Ben Striker."

"But I was never there."

I put my hand on Cody's shoulder. "I'll be down there in a few minutes to pick you up. I'm going to my office to get some paperwork. I'll represent you if you want me to."

"Yeah, it looks like I'm going to need a good attorney."

I arrived at the police station an hour later. Police Detective Tanner Truman was still questioning Cody. Chief Leland was standing in the hall watching through a window.

"I'm here to get my client, Chief," I said.

"It doesn't look good, Cam. He's not saying anything and the evidence is all against him."

"I told him not to say anything and the evidence is circumstantial at the best. His books are available to millions of readers. Anyone of them could be crazy enough to act out the crimes."

"While that's true, how many of them have mud that matches the crime scene on their shoes?"

"You and I for two, I think they were planted in his room while he was passed out," I said. "I didn't see any mud leading to his room."

"He could have carried them down the hallway."

148

"Why would he do that and then leave them in his room?"

"I don't know but you can have him after we finish the line-up," Leland said. "The guys from the shooting range are here."

"They can't possibly be sober. I refuse to let Cody stand up in front of a room full of drunks and be identified."

The chief stared at me. I think he was trying to size me up. He knew me well enough to realize I would have any charges dropped that were tied to the line-up.

"That same mud can be found all over the Keys," I said. "We would have to arrest everyone with muddy shoes. Now, I would like to get Cody and leave."

"Very well, Cam. I want him here in the morning for the line-up though."

"Fair enough, but you know the men have already disagreed with one another on the physical description of the man they were with. I believe they were too intoxicated at the time to be reliable."

"Just don't let him leave town before we get to the bottom of this," Leland said.

"He won't. He wants the answers too."

We left the station and went to the Hogs Breath for lunch. We needed to talk. I thought that maybe a more vibrant atmosphere would sharpen his senses.

"How are you feeling, Cody?" I asked.

"Tired," he said. "Maybe I *was* out all night."

"Maybe," I said, or drugged."

"Drugged?"

"Yes, you don't seem as upbeat as usual."

"Could someone have slipped something into your drink?"

"I guess so. We were at a few bars. We left our drinks on the table while we danced."

"You're a dancer?" I said smiling. The picture of him dancing wasn't a pretty one.

"Yeah, Olivia insists."

I thought about that. The nagging connection between Olivia and her husband wouldn't get out of my mind.

"Did you ever get her address?" I asked.

"No, but we could look it up," he said.

Cody pulled his cell phone out of his pocket and googled Timothy Harding in New York City. Thirty-five came up.

"Why didn't you do that before?" I asked.

"Didn't want to."

"Are there any married to an Olivia?"

He checked. "No."

I thought about that. "Check again without a city."

He did. "One hundred-seventeen in thirty-nine states."

"What about Olivia?"

He checked again. "Twenty professionals and hundreds of profiles."

"That's a lot," I said.

"Yeah. Too many to sift through."

"I'll have Jack check on it. He's good at that sort of thing."

We ate and listened to the guitarist for a while.

"You know," I said, "the Fest is almost over and there are still three murders left to commit. Someone is going to have to work fast to get them finished in two days."

"Yeah. The next one is someone tied behind a semi," Cody said.

I called Leland to see if he had anyone checking out trucks parked at docks.

"Sure, Cam. We have fifteen officers and three-hundred docks. We have them all covered."

I sensed a little sarcasm.

"I know it's overwhelming but it's all we have," I said.

"I'll do what I can," he said.

"Thanks," I said and hung up.

"A needle in a haystack," Cody said.

Chapter 26

Shaun Grease woke again. His hands were still bound behind him and his throat was dry. He had been locked in this hot cubicle for at least fifteen hours. The last thing he remembered was leaving Debbie and walking to his car. When he opened the door, someone hit him on the head and when he woke, he was here.

He pulled at his restraints once more but they wouldn't budge. He couldn't call for help because of the gag in his mouth. He felt his pockets behind him for his cell phone. His pockets were empty.

His eyes were adjusting to the darkness enough to know he was in the back of a cube van. Maybe a U-Haul truck or something similar. The rope holding his hands behind him was also tied to a rail in the truck, which prevented him from moving around inside.

Suddenly the back door rolled up into the ceiling and the bright sun shown in his eyes. Someone stepped into the van but Shaun couldn't see them because of the temporary blindness.

"Here," the man said in a tough voice.

The gag was removed and some kind of foul tasting food was jammed into his mouth. Next, water was poured on his lips. He opened his mouth enough to let some of the water seep in.

The gag was replaced and the man jumped out of the van pulling the door down with him.

What the hell, Shaun thought. Then things started to get blurry and Shaun passed out again. His last thought was, I've been drugged.

~***~

Cody and I drove around town aimlessly searching the docks for–for what? A guy tied up and laying behind a truck?

It didn't take long for us to realize we had little chance of finding the next victim before he showed up dead.

"I think we'd be better off trying to find who might be responsible for the murders, than the next victim," I said.

"Any leads?" Cody said.

"No," then I thought, "Maybe," I said.

Cody sat up straighter. "Who?"

"It's only a theory but it goes something like this," I said. "Every crime points to you."

"I'm your lead?" he said.

"No, you're my common denominator. It has to be someone close enough to you to know when you don't have an alibi. My guess is someone is trying to frame you for the murders."

"Yeah, we already figured that," he said.

"Okay, but we've tiptoed around it."

Cody looked at me blankly. I didn't want to say it aloud but I needed to.

"Olivia," I said.

"Olivia?"

"Yeah, she's the only one who knows where you are all the time."

Cody thought for a moment, and then said, "Or Emily."

"No, it couldn't be Emily. She was with me when one of the murders was committed."

Then I remembered what Kailey said. "All isn't as it seems." She said Emily was gone all night and returned in the morning as if she had never left.

"Yeah, maybe," I said.

"Maybe both," Cody said.

We rode in silence for a while.

"Does Olivia spend any time writing while you're here?" I asked.

"No, I haven't seen her write."

"Do you?"

"Every chance I get," he said.

"If she's working on a book, why isn't she writing?"

"Not everyone's as dedicated as I am. I love to write, to tell stories. Some people just write for the money. They can take a break and not be bothered by the fact their protagonist is in hibernation."

"What about Olivia? Does she just write for money?"

"I don't think so. She sounds passionate about her new book. She picked my brain more than once with questions about character development, plot twists, things like that."

"Does she read your books?"

"Yep, she's read all of 'em. She says they inspire her."

"What about Emily then? Does she write much?"

"I've walked in on her writing a few times. She's quick to close the laptop when I do. Some people don't want anyone to see their work until it's completed. I think she's one of those."

"Are you one of those?" I asked.

"I am," he said, "But Olivia reads it anyway. I gave her my password one night when I was a little inebriated."

I didn't know what my questions had to do with all this, but they seemed important. I would have to give it some thought.

"You know," I said, "I think we're going about this all wrong. We're out *here* looking for the next victim when we should be at the conference looking for the rest of the people who have worked on your books."

"Good thought."

"Make a list while I drive back to the hotel," I said.

Cody busied himself writing while I drove. If we could find the rest of the people who have worked with him, we might have a chance to stop the next crime before it happens.

I pulled into the lot just as Cody finished his list.

"This is all I have," he said handing me the paper.

I looked it over.

Debbie Lee: Line editor
Lonnie Harper: Animation
Shaun Grease: proofreader

"That's it?" I asked.

"Yeah, as far as I know, they're the only ones here that are still alive."

"It takes a lot of people to write a book," I said.

"Yeah, there are others, but they're not here."

"Well, let's go find these people."

When we entered the hotel lobby we were approached by a security guard. He didn't have a welcoming look on his face.

"Sorry Mister Paxton, I'm going to have to ask you to leave," he said in a stern tone.

I pulled my badge out and flashed it.

"We're working on the murder case involving several of your guests," I said. "Mister Paxton is a key investigator in the case. We need to be here."

"Those are my orders," he said bluntly.

"Are you impeding an investigation?"

"No, sir, just doing my job."

"Well, unless your job includes spending some time in jail, I'd think twice before blocking a murder investigation. As a matter of fact, we could use your help."

He puffed up at this. I thought he might.

"What do you need?" he said now changing his tone.

Chapter 27

We searched the seminars that were still in session with no luck in finding any of the guests on the list.

Standing in the lobby, Cody saw Lonnie Harper at the checkout desk. We approached him.

"Lonnie," Cody said. "Leaving already?"

Lonnie turned and recognized Cody. He extended his hand and they shook.

"Yeah, I have some deadlines to meet and if I'm going to be cooped up in a room I might as well be at home."

"It was good to finally meet you in person," Cody said. "I wish we could have spent more time together."

"Me too, Cody. You keep those books coming to me though and I'll keep drawing those pictures for ya."

"Alright," Cody said. "I'd like you to meet Cam Derringer."

We shook hands.

"I have a few questions, if you don't mind," I said.

"Sure."

"Has anyone approached you since you've been here? Maybe asking you to go out or come to their room or anything like that?"

He looked at me strangely. "What do you mean?"

"Actually, I don't know. Just anything out of the ordinary."

"Well," he scratched his head and looked around the room and blushed. "I was approached by a man. He asked me to come to his room. I think he's a writer."

"Do you know his name?"

"Eric," he said. "Eric Thompson."

Eric again, I thought.

I was about to ask him if he went to his room when he said defensively, "I didn't go. I'm not gay."

"That's okay, Lonnie. We didn't think you were. We're just trying to find anyone who might have worked on Cody's books and might be acting a little strange."

"Does this have anything to do with the murders?"

"Yes, it has a lot to do with the murders," Cody said.

"I've already made the connection to Cody," Lonnie said. "To be honest, that's part of the reason I'm leaving."

"I see," I said. "Can you think of anything else that might connect anyone to his books?"

He thought for a minute. "Not really, just Eric."

"Did you by any chance win this trip to the Murder Fest?"

"Yeah, I did. It came in the mail. I don't even know how I won, but the hotel reservation and the tickets for the Fest were both included."

"Have you seen, Debbie Lee or Shaun Grease?" I asked.

"Yeah, Debbie was in our discussion group this morning."

"Do you know where she is now?"

"No, but I have her phone number. I can call her."

"Do you mind?"

He dialed her number but there was no answer.

"Would you leave a message for her to call me?" I said.

I gave him the number and he left the message.

I thanked him and told him to be safe going home.

"I will. It's a short drive to Tampa," he said.

When he left, Cody and I split up and searched the hotel for Eric. We came up empty and met again in the lobby.

"Maybe he's gone home too," Cody said.

"He could have, but one thing bothers me. He doesn't seem gay. He's always after the girls. Why would he try to get Lonnie to come to his room?"

"Good question. Maybe to kill him."

My cell rang.

"Hello," I said.

"Mister Derringer, this is Debbie Lee. I had a message to call you.'

"Debbie, thanks for returning the call. I wanted to make sure you were alright."

"Why wouldn't I be?"

"I'm a PI working on the murders that have taken place here this week. It seems that all the victims had been working for Cody Paxton and since you were doing some of his editings, I just wanted to make sure."

"It sounds like you should be talking to Cody," she said.

"I have been," I said. "As a matter of fact, he's with me right now. He's also working on the case. That's how I knew to check on you."

"I'm on my way to the airport as we speak," she said.

"Good. I won't bother you again. Have a nice flight home."

"Thanks."

We were about to hang up when I remembered to ask her about Shaun.

"Debbie," I said. "Do you know Shaun Grease?"

"Yes, I do."

"Have you seen him today?"

"No, I haven't seen him since last night. We went to supper together then we came back to the hotel. He was going to go get a bottle of wine at the package store and bring it to my room, but he never showed up."

"What time was that?"

"Around eight. I figured he changed his mind. Is he okay?"

"As far as we know he is," I said.

"When you find him will you tell him to call me so I'll know he's okay?"

"Sure will, thanks for your help."

We hung up.

"Shaun's been missing since eight o'clock last night," I told Cody.

"That's not good. He could be dead by now."

"In your book, was it day or night when they found the body?"

"They found it in the morning. Pieces of the body were found on the highway, leading the police to the truck stop, where a part of the body was still cuffed to the trailer," Cody said.

I looked at Cody.

"What?" he said.

"You're sick."

"Yeah, I've been told that, but sick sells."

"Whoever is doing this could write a bestseller about it," I said.

"Yeah," Cody said, "They could call it, Murder Fest Key West."

I looked at him again.

"No, I'm not writing a new book," he said.

"Maybe someone is though."

Cody thought about that for a moment.

"Emily's writing something," he said.

"So is Olivia," I said.

We looked at each other now in silence.

"Nah," Cody said. "They wouldn't do that."

Chapter 28

We returned to the boat so I could let Walter out for a while. I fixed us both a drink and we sat at the table on the fantail.

"This is an impossible case," I said. "We know what's going to happen and now we might even know who it's going to happen to, but we can't get enough help to watch all the trucks coming and going."

"Not to mention, it might not even happen around here," Cody said. "It could be on up north on one of the other keys."

I thought about that. "We need to find the nearest truck stop. However, that will be after the fact. The body will already be…"

"Dismembered," Cody said.

"Yeah."

Cody pulled his phone out and googled truck stops near Key West. The closest one was in Miami.

"I don't think someone would go all the way to Miami to do this," I said. "They'd want it to be around here because they want it to look like you did it."

Walter ran onto the boat and came to me for petting. I patted his head and quit. He gave me a disappointed look and put his head on Cody's lap. Cody obliged him by rubbing his back.

"Maybe it's not a truck stop at all," I said. "Maybe more like a U-Haul or truck rental."

"Could be. Are there any around here?"

"Yeah, I've seen some," I said.

Cody checked his phone again. "There's four in Key West."

"You have the addresses?"

"Yep, let's go," he said.

We stood to leave and Walter bolted for the gate. I guess he's going with us.

We stopped at the nearest neighborhood dealer. We explained the situation and the guy let us check out all his trucks.

"Do you have any trucks in other locations?" I asked him.

"There are three other locations in Key West but I don't have anything to do with them," he said.

"I meant, do you have any rented out right now?"

"Oh yeah, there's always some rented."

"Are there any rented just for local use. Someone who is going to return it back here?"

"Let me check my records," he said and went into the office.

Cody and I stood in the parking lot and looked around at the trucks again.

"You know," I said, "if someone did rent a truck to drag a guy around, he wouldn't return it anyway."

"That's what I was thinking," Cody said, "but I thought maybe you had some grand idea."

163

"No."

The man returned with a list.

"These are the ones rented," he said and handed me the paper.

I looked it over.

"Would you be able to describe any of them?" I asked.

"Better than that," he said, "I have their pictures."

"Pictures?"

"Yeah, driver's license."

"Could we see them?"

"I guess, but I want to cover the numbers. I'll let you look at the pictures."

"Good enough," I said.

We looked over the pictures but didn't see anyone we recognized. This was a dead end.

We thanked him for his help and drove to the next store. We repeated the same scenario two more times after that.

Driving back to the boat we passed a house where a Penske truck was backed into the driveway. The back door on the truck was closed and the house looked deserted.

We decided to pull to the curb and check it out. Walter jumped out and ran to the nearest tree to relieve himself.

The truck had a lock on it so we knocked on the house door. There was no answer and a look in the window revealed an empty house.

I walked to the truck and banged on the back door. No sound came from inside.

"I don't know Cody. Maybe I should call the sheriff and see if he would come to check this out."

Cody pulled his phone out again and called 911.

"There's been a break-in at a house on East Street," he said, "308," and hung up.

"They'll be here in a minute," he said.

"You can't do that. They'll be pissed at me now and I have to live here."

Suddenly Walter started to bark and run around the truck. He stopped at the back door, jumped up putting his paws on the bumper and barked again.

"What is it, boy?" I said.

"We need to get that door open," Cody said.

I went to my car and searched through the trunk for something to break the lock. That's when I heard a shot ring out. I ducked.

Looking toward Cody I saw him putting his gun back in his pocket and opening the door.

I ran to the truck and looked in. There was a man bound and gagged at the front of the box. I jumped in and ran to him. He was breathing but he was unconscious.

"Call 911 again and order an ambulance," I said.

He did as I untied the man and pulled him out of the truck.

"Do you have a license to carry that gun?" I asked.

"Nope," he said.

"Give me the gun."

He handed it to me and I put it in my belt. I placed my gun in the car under the seat.

Cody was holding the man in a sitting position trying to wake him.

"It's Shaun Grease," he said

Shaun stirred but didn't wake.

"He's really out," Cody said.

Walter came over and licked Shaun on the face. I eased him away.

"Good boy, Walter," I said and patted him on the head.

Cody looked at me.

"What's wrong?" I said.

"Didn't anyone ever teach you how to pet a dog?"

"Well, I never had one before," I said.

He shook his head and told Walter, "Poor baby."

Walter licked Cody and gave me a dirty look.

The ambulance arrived along with the sheriff's deputy.

"Someone break in this house?" Deputy Parker asked.

I had talked to him a few times, but he has only been with the sheriff for about a year. He seemed dedicated to his job and all in all, not a bad guy.

"We don't know for sure," I said. "We were looking for a van or truck that might have been used to…"

"Yeah, yeah, yeah I know about it. What made you think this was the one?"

"We stopped to take a look and my dog went crazy running around barking. Thank goodness he did because the guy tied-up inside would have been dead in the morning."

He looked at Walter. Walter stared back.

The deputy inspected the truck. "How'd you get it open?"

"I shot the lock off," I said, knowing I would get in trouble for discharging a firearm in the city limits.

"Good job," he said.

"Thanks," I said.

"Do you know who lives here?" he asked.

"The house is empty. My guess they just parked the truck here to hide it in plain sight."

"Do you know the guy who was inside the truck?"

"I do," Cody said.

"Who are you?"

"Cody Paxton."

"You're the guy who wrote all the books the murders are from."

"I know it," Cody said.

Parker just looked at him.

"He's my proofreader," Cody said pointing at Shaun.

"How'd *you* know this truck was here?"

"We just happen to see it."

Parker stared at Cody again.

"You write some sick stuff," Parker said.

"I told ya," I said to Cody.

"Geez, guys. It's entertainment."

Parker looked at me and shook his head.

"Good job guys. We'll call you if we need anything," Parker said. "I'm going to try to find out who rented this truck and who owns this house."

"Thanks," I said. "Call me if you get anything."

"Sure," he said.

The ambulance left with Shaun. We decided we'd visit him in a few hours. Maybe he'd be awake and able to give us a clue as to who took him. Whoever it was expected him to die so maybe they didn't hide their identity.

"Now what?" Cody asked.

"Well, we saved a life. It's a good day."

"Yeah, but as far as the books go, that leaves the PI's daughter."

I called Diane.

"Hey, Cam," she said.

"I'd like for you to come to the boat. Can you be there in about an hour?"

"Sure," she said. "What's up?"

"I need to run something past you."

"See ya in an hour."

On the way back to the boat Walter laid his head in Cody's lap. I think he was trying to tell me I could be replaced.

When we were back at the boat, I took the opportunity to take a shower. Halfway through the shower, while the hot water was relaxing my muscles, the door opened and Emily stepped in.

A half hour later I was dressed and drinking a Wild Turkey on the lanai with Emily when Diane arrived.

I had a dilemma now. What I was going to tell Diane, I didn't want Emily to hear.

"Hi, guy's," she said stepping onto the boat. "Thought I'd stop by to see what's going on."

I was puzzled. Then I saw Cody behind her.

"Look who I found," he said.

Good boy, Cody. He gave Diane a heads up.

Emily stood and hugged her. "I just stopped by to see what was up myself," she said smiling at me.

We all sat at the table talking until Emily finished her drink.

"I've got to run," Emily said. "Have you guy's seen, Olivia?"

"Not since this morning," Cody said.

"I better go find her. We have an appointment to get our nails done."

"Maybe we can do a late supper," I said.

"We'll see," she said. "Give me a call."

I walked her to her car and thanked her for washing my back.

"Any time," she said. "I just felt the urge."

Chapter 29

Returning to the boat, I thanked Cody for telling Diane that Emily was here. It wouldn't have worked for Diane to ask why I wanted to see her in front of Emily.

"What's up, Cam?" Diane asked.

"I can't be sure but it looks like the next prologue concerns you and me," I said and told her about Shaun, and what was supposed to take place in the next book.

"You can't be sure that's aimed at you and me," she said.

"No, but who better?"

"I don't know. Maybe one of the police on the case," she said.

"Maybe," I said. "At any rate, I want to know you're safe and the best way to do that is to keep you with me."

"I can't stay with you. I have patients to see and a life to live."

I looked at her for a few seconds and said, "I liked it a lot better when you were a little girl and did what I told you to do,"

"Sorry, Dad, all grown up," she said holding her arms out.

"Well, I'm going to keep an eye on you anyway."

"Good. I'll feel safer that way."

"Will you at least sleep here on the boat?"

Diane thought it over, "Sure, but you're doing the cooking."

I felt a lot better but anything could happen to her during the day.

"I'm sorry you guys have to go through all this. I would have never written those books if I had known," Cody said.

"It's not your fault, Cody," I said. "Whoever is doing this would have found someone else's books to copy the murders from. There's someone out there that's sicker than you."

"Aw gee, thanks, Cam."

"That wasn't meant to be a compliment."

Diane rose from her chair and hugged Cody.

"Don't you listen to him," she said. "He's just jealous because his book failed after the first page."

"I'm fixing drinks. Who wants one?" I asked.

"I'll have one," Diane said.

"Cody?" I said.

"No thanks, one's enough," he said.

I thought that over and realized that I haven't seen Cody have more than one or two drinks while he was with me.

"Cody, have you cut back on the drinking?"

"Yeah, the doc said it would be a good idea."

"When was this?"

"A few months ago," he said.

"But when I picked you up at the police station, you were soused."

"I know. I must have slipped. I don't remember."

"Do you remember drinking a lot the other night when Ben Striker was killed at the shooting range?" I asked.

"Not really. Olivia and I were out dancing and I had maybe two beers."

"I'm thinking someone might be drugging ya, Cody."

"That's what it sounds like," Diane said. "Maybe we should have some blood work done on you to check for drugs."

"Nah, who'd drug me? I've only been around the girls and I know they're not doin' it."

"Maybe someone serving at the events. They might be giving you something that reacts to the alcohol you drink later."

"To what end?" Cody said. "What good would that do 'em?"

"They'd be able to frame you," Diane said.

"Still, It would have to be the girls. They know where I am all the time. They aren't strong or tough enough to have killed all these people."

"Yeah, it would have been hard for them to do," I said.

"Not if they had help," Diane said.

"True," Cody said. "But I know they don't have anything to do with it. I can judge character."

"Let's at least get the drug test," I said.

"Alright," Cody said. "If you say so."

Diane made a call to a friend and set up an appointment in one hour.

"I'll take you to get it done," Diane said. "We'll be back in a few hours."

"I'll treat you to ice-cream afterward," Cody said.

"You're on."

When they left, I decided I'd take the time to write down all the events and see if we're overlooking something obvious.

I took my billfold out and laid it on the dresser since I wasn't going anywhere. That's when I remembered the waitress giving me her number. I was curious as to what she wanted. I decided to call her.

I unfolded the note again. *Susan Daily.* I was sure I didn't know her. I called the number.

"Hello," she answered.

"Is this Susan Daily?"

"Yeah," she said hesitantly.

"This is Cam Derringer," I said. "You gave me your number the other night."

"I thought you'd never call," she said sensually.

"Do I know you from somewhere?"

"You do now," she said.

"I'm sorry," I said, "I'm at kind of a loss. Did you want me to call you for a reason?"

"Yes. You tried to get to me four nights ago but you were turned away. I don't think you were welcome."

"I don't recall."

"The hotel. Remember the murder scene?"

I thought. "You were the girl in the window."

"Very good."

"I'm sorry for not calling earlier," I said.

"Story of my life."

"Well, I was going to ask you if you saw anything the night of the murder but I guess you would have gone to the police by now."

"Not necessarily. I don't much care for the police."

"You did see something?" I asked.

"Not much, it was dark. I did see someone standing under the Banyan tree and the girl walking past. They talked for a minute and then another person met them. This one was carrying a bag. The three of them started to fight. The girl went down and the other two were on top of her for a minute. Before they left, they hung the bag on the door and took another bag with them. I didn't know they killed her until the next day."

"You saw all that and didn't tell anyone?" I said.

"I told you."

"Would you recognize any of them?"

"No, It was dark and raining hard," she said.

"Nothing you can add that might help?"

"Well, the first one, the one under the tree, might have been a woman."

"Can I meet with you sometime to go over this again?" I asked.

"You can meet with me anytime, Cam."

I hung up and made that drink I missed earlier. This was getting to be complicated.

Chapter 30

I opened my notebook to review all that had happened. Maybe there was something in the timeline I had missed.

My cell rang but I didn't recognize the number, "Hello?"

"Cam, this is Wanda."

Crazy Wanda I thought. I didn't even know her last name.

"Hello, Wanda."

"I can't find Dave."

"What do you mean?"

"We were sitting in my backyard having a drink when his phone rang. He said, "yep-nope-okay-right now?-okay and bye" then he told me he'd be right back and walked to the front yard. Half an hour later, I walked around front and he was gone. I called his cell and I could hear it ring. It was laying in the grass."

"Do you know who he was talking to?"

"No idea."

I thought a minute then said, "Dave told me he might have pissed off the wrong people, do you know what he meant?"

She hesitated.

"Wanda?"

"He might have been talkin' about a few weeks ago when he was fishin' on the beach."

I waited. "And?"

"Well, this guy wanted to buy some pot from Dave. Dave gave him a bag and the guy paid him."

I waited again.

"So," I said. "Why would that piss the guy off?"

"Well, Dave might have gotten the bag of pot mixed up with a bag of tea he had in his cooler. They look the same."

"Dave's passing off tea for pot? How many times do you think he might have made this mistake?"

"Maybe a few, but usually only to tourist."

"Who was the guy he did it to this time?"

"I think it was one of the Chastain brothers, Charlie," she said.

"Charlie Chastain? He's the closest thing we have to the mafia around here."

"Yeah, I know."

"Dave would know better than to do that. He knows Charlie."

"He needed the money. He kind of made a bad bet on some dumb horse with Olan."

"Olan Chastain?"

"Yeah."

"Jesus. What's wrong with Dave?"

"It wasn't his fault. He was drunk."

I knew the Chastain family. I defended Sly Chastain on a burglary charge 10 years ago. He broke into a house and was caught by the owner, or I should say, caught by the owner's Doberman. The dog chewed him up pretty bad. His sentence was reduced when he cooperated with the police on a murder case. He was with a man who shot the clerk in a liquor store robbery. The guy died a week later. In court, Sly testified, "Yes, I was with him, but I didn't know he was going to rob the store. Before I could stop him, he killed the guy so we ran. He said he'd kill me if I ever told anyone."

We knew this was bullshit, but we had no proof Sly had any intent to rob the store. He helped nail the lid on the case and the other man is doing life in prison.

"How much does Dave owe Olan?"

"Fifteen-thousand."

"How long has Dave been missing?"

"Since yesterday, around noon."

"I'll see what I can do, Wanda. You call me if you hear from him."

"I will, right away," she said, her voice cracking.

"We'll find him," I said but wasn't too sure we would. These guys have gotten harder and more ruthless over the years and no matter what they're accused of, they get off scott free.

"Thanks, Cam," she said sincerely.

"How did they know Dave was with you?"

"I don't know."

When we hung up, I scrolled through my contacts and found Sly's number. I called him.

"Cam Derringer," he answered. "To what do I owe the pleasure?"

"Hello Sly. I'm calling about a friend who's missing."

"Do you want to hire me to help you find him?"

"Are you in the business of finding people now?"

"I can find anyone for, let's say, twenty-thousand."

"What's wrong with fifteen-thousand," I said.

"Cost of living."

"I see. Would the person I'm looking for be alive when we find him?"

"Depends on how long it takes us to find him."

"What if we start looking right away and he shows up in, let's say, an hour?"

"I don't think I could find him that quickly. He has to be missing for at least a few days."

"Why's that?"

"Maybe he needs to confess his sins or something."

"I want him back, unharmed," I said. "And I want him back today."

"I'll call you tomorrow if I find him," Sly said and hung up.

Chapter 31

An hour later, when Diane and Cody returned I had my head buried in my notebook. The more I looked at the facts the more Olivia played into it. The problem is, if it's her, she has to have help. That's where Emily comes into the picture. But I'm not sure Olivia and Emily are strong enough to pull some of these murders off. And, what about the guy at the shooting range? That surely wasn't one of them.

"The test results will be back tomorrow," Diane said.

"Good," I said. "For now, let's don't say anything in front of Olivia and Emily. They might not have anything to do with this, but they don't need to know all the details anyway."

"Not a problem," Cody said.

"And it might be a good idea if you didn't drink around them."

"I'll do my best," Cody said. "But you're wrong about them."

"I hope so."

Diane said her goodbyes and promised she would return before bedtime.

I called Emily who said she just met up with Olivia. They had missed their nail appointment but they would be happy to have supper with us.

We picked the girls up at six. I had told them to dress for a fancy restaurant but I didn't expect them to look this exquisite.

Emily was dressed in a low-cut black dress that showed off her cleavage and her shapely, bronzed legs.

A simple diamond hung on a short gold chain from her neck with matching earrings.

Olivia was dressed in a similar dress only in red. The contrast of the two women was enough to perk up all your senses.

Cody and I stood silently staring. The girls looked at each other and smiled.

"That's the reaction we were going for," Emily said.

"You both look..." I tried to say.

"Thanks, I think," Olivia said.

Cody and I looked at each other and then we each looked at our own clothes. I had on white slacks a pink shirt, untucked, and a light blue sports coat.

Cody was dressed in khaki slacks an alabaster shirt, also untucked, and a beige sports coat.

We thought we looked pretty good until we saw the girls.

Cody hugged Olivia lightly as if he didn't want to break anything.

"You're beautiful," he said.

I kissed Emily on the cheek, held out my arm and said, "Shall we?"

Emily took my arm as we walked to the car.

"Where are we going?" she asked.

"We're going to Sunset Key to Latitudes. It's located in the Westin Hotel."

After a short boat taxi ride, we walked a block to the hotel and entered the restaurant. I had been here several times and never tired of the view.

We were escorted to a table that I had requested in the bar area where a wall of glass offered a spectacular view of the palm tree strewn beach.

Cody and I pulled the ladies cane back chairs out and seated them before taking our own places.

"This is beautiful," Emily said.

"It's my favorite," I said.

Olivia just said, "Wow," under her breath.

I had the Tuna while Emily opted for Lobster. Olivia ordered Salmon and Cody, Steak.

We had several bottles of wine with our meal, but Cody had only one glass and a light dessert of chocolate mousse.

"Shall we have a seat on the patio for an after dinner drink?" I asked.

They thought that was an excellent idea.

Our drinks arrived and I kept a watch on Cody's. I don't know what I was expecting, but I couldn't help myself.

We left an hour later returning the girls to their hotel.

"I'm sorry to leave such lovely company," I said, "But I have an early appointment in the morning."

"Thank you for the magical evening, Cam," Emily said. "I'm going to miss you when I return to New York."

"I'll miss you too," I said and kissed her.

I finally pulled away knowing if the kiss lasted any longer it would carry on into the morning hours.

Diane was sitting on the lanai with Walter when we arrived.

"Don't you two look nice," she said.

"Latitudes," I said.

"And you already ditched the ladies?"

"I'm sure there'll be a time I'll be sorry for that."

I removed my jacket and laid it over a chair. I looked at Cody who was just standing there.

"Are you going to get comfortable?" I asked.

He looked around avoiding eye contact. "Well, I know you don't want me to, but I told Olivia I would pick her up and we'd go listen to music for a while."

"Cody, do you think that's wise?"

"I just don't think they have anything to do with it," he said.

"I can't stop you, but I think it's a bad idea."

"I'll be careful, Cam."

With that, he left.

Chapter 32

I was up early the next morning. I checked Cody's room. He hadn't come home but I didn't really think he would. I woke Diane because I knew she had an early appointment.

I made breakfast while she showered and dressed.

"Here ya go," I said as she entered the kitchen. "I'm holding up my part of the bargain by cooking."

"Smells good, Cam," she said while placing a stack of pancakes on her plate.

We dug in while making small talk.

"You'll be back here again tonight, won't you?" I asked.

"I'll be here. I need to go home for a while first but I'll be here later."

"Good."

I kissed her on the cheek as I cleared the plates.

"See ya," she said as she left.

I decided to go for a run while I had the chance. I called Jack. He met me on Roosevelt Boulevard and we ran toward the airport.

I filled him in on Shaun and shared my suspicions about the girls.

"You mind if I do a little investigating on Emily?" he asked.

"I was hoping you would," I said.

Jack is good at digging deep into people's pasts. If there were something to find, he would find it.

We passed the airport and kept running. When we arrived at Smathers Beach, we sat on a bench and watched the girls running past. There were usually a few that were a pleasure to watch.

I checked my cell phone.

"Expecting an important call?" he asked.

"Hopefully," I said and told him about Dave.

"That's not good, Cam. They don't need the twenty-thousand and they don't take kindly to people ripping them off."

"Yeah, I know. That's what bothers me."

"If we don't hear from them by this evening we'll pay them a visit," Jack said.

"Not we," I said, "me."

"Too risky to go alone."

"We'll see when the time comes."

We sat a few more minutes.

"Do you think Diane's in any danger?" he asked.

"She's staying with me at night until we get this solved," I said.

"She can stay with me," he said.

"She's fine where she is."

"Just sayin'."

I'm aware that Diane and Jack are an item, but anytime I can intervene a bit, I do. I love them both but Jack has a past.

"You ready?" Jack asked.

"Sure," I said even though I was starting to feel my fifty-three years.

Jack was much younger and sometimes I think he pushes me for my own good.

We ran back and split-up at Highway 1.

"I'll call you with what I find," he said. "You call me as soon as you hear from Sly."

When I got home, I took a shower after letting Walter run a little.

I needed a break from–everything. I decided to take Walter to a new "Doggy Bar" I'd heard about on Higgs Beach. It was the kind of place I would never go to before I adopted Walter.

The bar had no walls and a thatched roof. It looked like most of the other bars in Key West other than inside there was a wall of wooden beads everywhere you looked. The bar was divided into cubicles. Each had a table surrounded by the beads. A pretty, young, Mexican waitress escorted Walter and I to one such cubicle, pulled the beads aside and motioned us in.

There was a ceiling fan inside the cubicle. With the bead walls, the air circulated and the area was actually cool. A clean water bowl and food bowl sat on the sand floor next to the table.

The beads were spaced so as not to obstruct the view of everyone else in the bar or the beach. It kept each dog to itself but not alone. I liked it.

"Uno Cerveza," I said to the waitress.

"Alto?"

"Si."

She smiled and left to get my beer. My words are usually correct, but my accent is always–good ole boy, conch style.

She returned with a tall beer and set it on the table. There was ice on the glass. She also had a pitcher of cold water that she poured into Walters's water bowl and a pouch of some kind of treat, which she placed in the food bowl.

"Hola, Walter," she said rubbing his head.

Walter licked her hand.

"You know Walter?" I said.

"Si, Walter is an old friend of mine. How is Dave?"

"Dave is Dave," I said. "I'm keeping Walter for him for a while. He's going through a few things."

"Crazy Wanda," she said.

"Pretty much."

"Would you like something to eat?"

"Not yet, thanks. I think I'll enjoy my beer first."

"Hola," she said, patted Walter again and left.

I looked at Walter, "You are such a stud." He smiled.

There was a conch sitting in the cubicle next to mine. I could tell by his accent when he ordered. He had some kind of a short-haired dog on his lap. Instead of eating out of the dog bowl, the dog was eating off the man's plate.

The guy was slightly overweight and looked a little unkempt.

Two tables over I saw a young lady come in and sit down. She didn't have a dog. I couldn't see her face, but she had a killer body.

I sipped my beer. Walter crunched a dog treat.

Another man entered and sat at the table with the conch.

"Hey Pete," he said as he sat.

"Hey Tommy," the other said.

"Hi there Princes," Tommy said to the dog.

The dog continued to lick the plate.

"What's new?" Pete said.

"I had to get away from that stupid kid," Tommy said. "Thought I'd come to see if you were here."

"Here I am," Pete said.

"What's wrong with the kid?"

"He's stupid. He won't do anything I tell him to do."

"Maybe you ask too much of him."

"I'm done with him," Tommy said.

Pete lowered his voice but I could still hear him, "You shouldn't have bought him then."

Now both men were whispering, "I think I might shoot him."

"No, you can't do that."

"He deserves it," Tommy said.

They quit talking while the waitress delivered their beers.

I thought back to the night when I was in the fifth grade and saw my classmate Susie, being held by her father while our schoolteacher was standing outside her window watching. She was naked and helpless. I found out later that her father had ties to a sex trafficking ring.

I started dating Susie in our senior year of high school. Four months later, I killed her father with a baseball bat only seconds after he killed Susie with his fists. My only regret was that I didn't kill him seconds before he killed her.

Am I listening to another sex trafficking situation now?

Walter sensed my mood and stiffened. He raised his head and looked around and then at me. I patted him on the head.

"I'll buy him from you," Pete said.

"What would you do with 'em?"

"I could tie him up in the backyard and let him eat the grass," Pete said.

"I don't think your neighbors would take kindly to a goat in your yard," Tommy said.

I let out a breath and smiled. "A goat," I said to Walter.

Sensing things were okay Walter went back to his bowl.

The waitress went to the woman a few tables away to take her order. She gave her order and Walter jumped up.

"What's wrong boy," I said.

He looked around excitedly. Then he ran out through the curtains and straight to the woman who just ordered. He put his front paws on her lap.

Oh, crap, Walter. I jumped up too and went after him, apologizing on my way to her table.

"He's fine," Kailey said petting Walter on the head.

Chapter 33

"Kailey," I said pulling her from her chair and kissing her. "What are you doing here?"

"Actually," I never left. "It seems I *am* still obsessed with you."

I kissed her again. I couldn't get enough of her.

Walter kept jumping on her also. Everyone loved Kailey.

"If you didn't leave, why didn't you stay with me?" I asked.

"You have a new girlfriend."

"Not really," I said. "We've just dated a little. She's going back to New York in a couple of days."

"I wouldn't count on that," she said.

"Why?"

"There's no record of her ever living in New York, or anywhere else as far as that goes."

"You checked?"

"Yes Cam, I was worried about you and with all the murders…"

"You didn't find her anywhere?"

"I found a few Emily Chloros's, but none of the pictures matched."

"You think she's lying about her identity then?"

"It seems so."

"She said you had drinks with her the other day," I said.

"I wanted to check her out a little closer."

"And?"

"She seems okay, but Olivia...." She shrugged her shoulders.

"Jack's checking in to her past."

I kissed her again and Walter licked her.

"Boy, there sure are some horny men in Key West," she said looking at us.

"You'll have to excuse Walter," I said. "He can't help himself. Will you join us in our cubicle?"

"Will I be safe?"

"No."

"Okay."

We sat and the waitress brought Kailey's drink. I ordered some food.

"Here's what I found out," she said. "Emily doesn't live in New York and she has never published a book."

"She's just starting."

"Okay, but Olivia has published one. It ranked number five on Amazons best seller list."

"I didn't know that. Cody said she hadn't published anything yet."

"Yes, it's a nonfiction book about a man in Georgia who killed six family members and then himself. They think she actually embellished a little on the facts because some of the events only the murderer would have known."

"How'd she do that?"

189

"She knew gruesome details that the police never released. The murders spanned over a two-week period. The book is called, 'The Final Victim.'"

I sat staring. She continued.

"The surprising spin to the whole story is that she managed to release the manuscript only one week after the murders, while it was still fresh in everyone's mind."

"That doesn't seem possible," I said.

"It's not. The police finally questioned her. She wouldn't give up her source."

"How the hell?"

"And you know, she's married?"

"Yes, I knew that, but they don't get along. I think they're separated."

"That I don't know."

"Thanks for the information," I said.

"I'm just watching out for my man," she said.

"Are you going to come to the boat and stay with me?"

"Not yet," she said. "I have a very comfortable suite. I want to be able to move around a while without anyone knowing I'm here."

"You're not going to do something crazy, are you?"

"Cam, you know me better than that," she said and giggled.

Yeah right. I know of a few people she's killed and at least one she had an assassin kill.

"Please be careful," I said.

"Where's Diane?"

I told her about the next book in the series and that Diane was safe with me at night.

"That's why I asked. I read the prologue to the next book. It makes sense to me that it could be you and Diane."

"Cody and I found the guy they were going to tie behind the truck. The police left the truck in the driveway and are watching it. No one has returned to claim it yet. I think they might have to find another victim now."

"That gives you another day. They seem to want to follow the books."

"Unless they already have the stage set for the finale," I said.

"I think they'd cancel it until they drag someone behind the truck and if it has to be someone tied to Cody's books, that doesn't leave many people."

"It doesn't leave anyone as far as I know," I said.

"What are you going to do next?" she asked.

"I'm going to the hospital to talk to Shaun in a few hours. Maybe he saw his captors. They thought he was going to die so they might have been careless."

"Good idea. Will you call me afterward?" she said laying her hand on mine.

"I want to be with you," I said.

"We'll be together soon," she said and kissed me again.

Our food came and we made small talk as we ate. Walter indicated he had to relieve himself so I took him to a designated spot. It was a good thing I did.

When we returned, Kailey was gone. She's a mysterious woman and I love her.

I stopped at the hospital to see Shaun. I left the window down and told Walter I'd be right back.

There was an armed guard outside his room. He was a rookie who I'd seen around but never really talked to.

"Hello," I said shaking his hand and introducing myself.

"Can I talk to Shaun yet?" I asked.

"The chief said you'd probably stop by, but he's not in the room right now. They just took him down for tests."

"Is he conscious?"

"In and out. He hasn't said anything yet though," he said.

"I'll wait for a few minutes. Maybe he'll be awake when they bring him back."

I got a cup of coffee from the machine and sat in the waiting room where I had a view of Shaun's room.

I was reading the newspaper when someone said, "Cam."

I looked up to see Julie, a nurse I'd had the pleasure to have dinner with one evening.

"Julie," I said as I stood. "How are you?"

She just looked at me for a few seconds and said, "Lonesome," rather sarcastically.

Even though she's a beautiful young woman, we didn't exactly hit it off. Our politics are the extreme opposite and she liked to argue them, something I never do. I thought it was better if we didn't date.

I didn't know what to say.

She smiled, "I'm just bustin' your balls, Cam," she said.

I still didn't know what to say.

"What are you doing here?" she asked.

"I came to see Shaun Grease," I said.

"Yeah, the guy they brought in yesterday."

"Right, they took him down for tests. I'm just waiting for him to come back."

"Tests?" she said. "I don't think so. I took him for some tests at six o'clock this morning. He should be back in his room."

I wondered if the rookie had left his station and not seen Shaun return.

"Would you mind checking for me?" I asked.

"Sure," she said. "If you take me to supper tonight."

I could feel myself turning red. She laughed again, "Cam, you need to sharpen your sense of humor. Actually, I'm taken now. You missed your opportunity."

"You enjoy this, don't you?"

She laughed again, "I'll be right back."

I watched her go to Shaun's room, open the door and step in. She came back out immediately and walked to the nurse's station. She picked up a folder and looked through it. She laid the folder back down and went to the rookie and talked to him for a minute. She went back to the phone and made a call.

When she hung up, she looked alarmed. I went to the desk.

"What's wrong?" I asked.

"He's not here. They haven't had him back down in neurology and no other doctors have requested any tests."

We both stepped over to the rookie.

"What did they tell you when they took Shaun away?" I asked him.

"They said he was scheduled for tests," he said panic in his voice.

"How long ago was this?"

"Maybe fifteen minutes. Am I in trouble?" he said.

"That, I don't know."

I gave Julie my number and told her to call me if they find him.

"I've got to go," I said hurrying down the hall toward the exit.

As I was going out the door, an orderly was wheeling a gurney in.

"Where did you get that?" I said pointing at the gurney.

"Some jerk left it out in the parking lot," he said.

"Did you see who it was?"

"No, it was just sitting there next to the curb."

Chapter 34

I ran to the car and had to push Walter over to his side so I could get in. I started it and sped out of the lot. When I got to the street, I stopped. I had no idea which way to go. I called Jack.

"Would the cop recognize them if he saw them again?" Jack asked.

"I don't know. I didn't hang around long enough to question him," I said.

"I'll call the police to see if they know anything yet. Maybe you should go get Cody and search for a truck again. I don't know what else to do."

"There's not much we can do," I said. "Call me."

I drove to the boat. I tried to call Cody on the way. He didn't answer. I hoped he was at the boat.

Walter jumped out and ran to his favorite spot. He's getting old. He can't hold it long.

On the way up the dock, we were attacked by Hank. He clamped down on my flip-flop again. Walter just looked at him and then me and then back at Hank.

"Hank!" Stacy yelled. "Sorry, Cam."

I bent down and rubbed Hanks back. He forgot about the flip-flop and rolled over for more petting.

Stacy came down to the dock and picked him up.

"Bad boy!" she said.

"Don't worry about it," I said. "I keep extra flip-flops on the boat."

"I'm taking him to obedience school when he gets a little older."

"Have you seen Cody this morning?" I asked her.

"No. I haven't seen anyone on the dock today except you and Diane."

"Thanks," I said and patted Hank on the head, but his attention was on Walter now.

I went to the boat, opened the door and called for Cody, just in case. No answer.

I kicked off my slobbery flip-flops and went inside. Walter laid down on the lanai.

I went to the bedroom, got my gun and strapped the holster to my belt.

When I returned to the lanai, Walter was chewing on my flip-flop. He had the strap torn off already. When he looked up at me, the shoe dangled from his mouth.

"Bad boy!" I said.

He lowered his head and dropped the shoe. *Great, now Hank's teaching Walter bad habits.*

I opened the door and pointed inside, looking at Walter. He slinked in.

I got out his food and noticed his water bowl was missing. He lowered his head again and went into the living room. He returned with his bowl in his mouth. He knew I was mad.

I filled his bowl and set it down next to the food. He sat and waited patiently for me to move away.

"Come here," I said.

He walked slowly to me. I hugged him and rubbed his back. He perked up and licked me. I couldn't stay mad at him.

"I'll be back in a few minutes," I said. "Don't eat anything other than your food."

I decided to go to the hotel to see if Cody was there. I called Emily on the way. I didn't get an answer from her either. Where was everyone?

I knocked on the door of Emily and Olivia's room. It was held open by the security bar. I eased it open.

"Emily? Olivia? Hello."

No one was there. There was a laptop on the table. It was open so I moved the mouse. The screen lit up and text appeared.

It looked as if someone had been writing a novel. I read a few lines looking over my shoulder nervously, feeling guilty.

The words jumped out at me.

When the police finally found the torso, it was still chained to the truck bumper, they could barely recognize Shaun Grease.

"What the hell," I said aloud. "Emily?"

"Sir, what are you doing?" I heard from behind me.

I turned to see a woman from housekeeping giving me a suspicious look.

"The women from this room, have you seen them?" I asked.

"Sir you need to leave before I call security," she said.

"Look, it's very important. They might be in great danger."

"I haven't seen them," she said pointing to the door. "Now go."

I left the room and searched the hotel lobby and dining room. They weren't here.

I saw Henry Strait in the lobby and approached him.

"Hello, Cam."

"Henry," I said. "Have you seen Emily, Olivia or Cody this morning?"

"No, not since last night. I saw Olivia and Cody leaving together."

"What time was that?"

"Late, probably around eleven-thirty."

"What about Emily?"

"No, she wasn't with them," he said. "Is everything alright?"

"Yeah, would you tell them to call me if you see any of them?"

"Will do," he said.

"Thanks."

I left the hotel puzzled. *How did Emily know about Shaun and why was she writing a book about him being killed already?*

I called Chief Leland to see if he had any leads on Shaun.

"We have a team looking for him Cam, but it was lucky you found him the first time."

"Yeah, I know. I think you should widen that search to Cody and Olivia also."

"Why's that?"

"I think they might be in danger. I just found evidence that Emily knows about Shaun and has already written his death scene in a novel."

"Emily?"

"Yes."

Leland paused.

"Cam, don't worry about Emily. She's not the one doing this," Leland said.

"How do you know that?"

"Just take my word for it."

"But the laptop, I saw it." Then I figured it out, "Olivia?" I said.

"Probably."

"And Emily?"

"She's Thomas Barron's sister. He was accused of killing his family in Macon, Georgia and then himself."

"Yes, I know about the murders," I said.

"Emily's managed to get close to Olivia to find out how she knew so much about the murders."

"How'd you know all this?"

"The Macon Police Department and the FBI are watching Olivia's movements. They don't have enough proof to assign on-site personnel to the case yet, but they did notice that Emily was traveling with her. They contacted me and gave me the identity of Emily Barron and Olivia Harding. They hinted that if I had the personnel, it would be a good idea to watch them both."

"You could have told me."

"No I couldn't," he said. "We didn't have any reason to link these murders with the family murder, suicide."

"Do you know where any of them are now?" I asked.

"No, we haven't heard from anyone today."

"Do you think Oliva is actually behind this?"

"I do now since you told me about the laptop."

"Thanks, Chief. I'll call if I hear anything," I said and hung up.

Chapter 35

I haven't seen Cody, Emily or Olivia now for twenty-four hours. I was starting to worry and the Author Fest was ending today. A lot of people would be leaving and along with them any suspects we might come up with.

I had no idea what to do next. I was driving down Roosevelt when my phone rang again. I didn't recognize the number.

"Hello," I said.

"Cam."

"Kailey," I recognized, "what's up?"

"Can you meet me for supper in half an hour?"

"Where?"

"How about Louie's Backyard?"

"Great," I said. "Is something wrong?"

"A few things I want to tell you."

"I'm on my way. Love ya.'

"Love you too," she said.

Louie's is a top-notch restaurant serving Caribbean-American food. Inside are white tablecloths, and outside is a picturesque deck overlooking the beach. I chose outside at the corner of the deck. Kailey was only five minutes behind me.

I stood and kissed her as I seated her next to me.

The waiter came and took our order. We made small talk while our drinks were served, and we placed our food order.

"This must be important," I said.

"Yes, it is."

I put my hand on hers. "Tell me."

"Olivia's husband is here."

"Here in Key West?"

"Yes."

"I need to tell Cody."

"I think it's too late for that," she said.

"What do ya mean?"

"Have you seen Cody lately?"

I told her the whole story about Cody and the girls disappearing and Shaun being taken from the hospital.

"And," I said, "Emily is Thomas Barren's sister."

"The one who murdered his family?" Kailey said.

"Yeah."

"Now it makes sense. That's why Emily left your bed in the middle of the night. She was trying to keep an eye on Olivia."

"I don't know any other reason a girl would leave my bed in the middle of the night," I said and then realized I shouldn't have.

Kailey got a stern look on her face. "Don't push your luck," she said.

"Sorry, that was meant as a joke."

"Anyway, you know Olivia's husband."

"I do?"

My mind fought to bring up the identity of her husband. I couldn't think of anyone. I stared at her blankly.

"Eric Thompson," she said.

The waitress brought our food. Kailey pushed it around the table and thanked the waitress while I just stared at her.

"Eric?" I said. "That can't be. He's seen Olivia with Cody and didn't do anything. Cody even knocked him out."

"And he didn't press charges, did he?"

"No."

"They needed Cody out of jail."

"So, Eric and Olivia are working together."

"They're murdering all these people just to write another book," she said.

"Diane," I said. "She and I are next. I need to stop them."

"Diane's staying with you at night," Kailey said.

"What about during the day? What about right now," I said hearing panic in my voice.

"She's good," Kailey said and looked up. "Here she is now."

"Hey guys," Diane said as she walked to our table. "What's up?"

I stood and kissed her and seated her at the table.

"You asked her to come here?" I said to Kailey.

"Yes, she did," Diane answered for her.

"I knew you needed to see she was safe from Olivia," Kailey said.

"Olivia," Diane said. "What's she got to do with this?"

"She's the one who's been murdering all these people," I said. "along with her husband, Eric."

"Eric? Do you know him?"

"Yes, he's the one Cody knocked out at the fest."

"Shit," Diane said.

"Yeah, shit," Kailey said. "Now the two of you need to be kept safe. The best way is for you to stay together for another day or two."

"I'll have Jack stay with her," I said. "I have to find them and hopefully Cody and Emily."

"My guess is Cody, Emily, and Shaun, are being held by Olivia and Eric," Kailey said.

"If that's the case, they're in a lot of danger," I said.

"Yes, they are. They could be dead by tomorrow."

"I hope Cody has figured it out by now," I said

"If he has," Kailey said. "That might not be a good thing."

I called Jack and naturally, he said he'd love to keep Diane close by his side for the next few days. I was surprisingly relieved.

"If it's that important to them to find Diane and me, they won't stop until they do."

"I'll be safe with Jack," Diane said. "You just be careful on the street."

Jack arrived the same time our dessert did. He ordered a piece of pie and a glass of water.

"I'm glad to see you're not drinking alcohol," I said.

"Not tonight. I'm going to keep this precious cargo safe," he said and kissed Diane.

"We can stay at my place," Diane said.

"Probably safer at mine," Jack argued.

"We'll see."

We finished our meal and left. We all agreed to keep in touch through the evening. I walked Kailey to her car.

"Would you like to stay with me tonight?" I asked.

"Yes, very much, but I have things to do," she said.

"I don't like it, you being out there alone looking for murderers."

"I'll be safe. You stay safe too. They don't know me, but they'll be looking for you."

I kissed her goodnight. I hoped it wouldn't be the last time.

I called Chief Leland and filled him in on Eric.

"Do you know where Eric's staying?" he asked.

"He was staying at the Caribbean Palm Village. I don't know if he's checked out or not."

"I'll send some men over there."

When we hung up, I tried Emily's cell phone and got no answer. I then tried Cody again and still no answer.

I returned to the boat to let Walter out. It was a good thing I did. My patio door was open. Someone had been here, or they were here now. I didn't see Walter anywhere. I pulled my gun and stepped inside.

Chapter 36

A search of the boat yielded no intruders and nothing seemed to be disturbed. Still no Walter though. That had me worried. My cell rang.

"Cam, is that you on your boat?"

It was Stacy.

"Yes, it is. Why?"

"I thought I saw someone there about a half hour ago. I was just getting Walter some water and was going to call you to let you know he was here. I thought it was just you letting him out until I saw you come home."

"Walter's with you?"

"Yeah, he came running to my door a few minutes ago wanting in."

"He's a great watchdog. Someone's been here," I said.

"Then it wasn't you," she said.

"How many did you see?"

"Just one, I think. A man."

"Thanks. Can you watch Walter for the night? I have some things I need to do."

"I know what that means. You're in trouble again, aren't you?

"I'll be fine, but if you see anyone on my boat, lock your door and call me."

"I will. Don't worry about Walter, he and Hank are playing."

Oh no, more bad habits.

"Thanks, I owe you," I said.

"Steak and wine should do it."

"You're on."

"Where're we going?" Cody asked.

"Let's hit one more bar and then I have a special place I want to show ya," Olivia said.

"I've already had more to drink than I have in months. Why don't we just go back to our room?"

"Awe, come on. Don't be a party pooper. I want to dance."

Cody relented although he was not in any shape to be dancing. However, he did want to please Olivia in any way he could.

"Why don't we just stay in Key West?" he asked as they were driving north up Highway 1.

"I thought it would be nice to venture out a little. We've been everywhere there. Besides, I know of a really cool place on Sugarloaf Key. You'll love it."

"Okay then, let's go," he said.

Olivia pulled into a small neighborhood bar a block off the highway. The neon sign flashed green and red broadcasting 'THE ANCHOR CLUB'.

They parked on the side of the building and went in.

The jukebox was playing reggae music. There were two couples dancing, making moves Cody knew would be impossible for him to do. The rhythm probably wouldn't allow any of the moves he knew.

"Are you sure you want to dance to this?" he asked.

"Yeah, let's give it a try, but a drink first," she said.

They took a table between the bar and the dancefloor. There weren't many people in the bar. He counted four couples and a table of five older men plus the four dancing and now he and Olivia. There was also a table in a dark corner with one man who might be waiting for someone.

"I think I could write a book about this place," Cody said.

"Really? What would you call it?"

Cody thought a minute, "Sawdust and Suckers" he said.

Olivia laughed. "It's not that bad."

"Yeah, we'll give it a chance and then see."

The waitress took their order and returned a minute later with their drinks. Cody pulled his wallet out to pay and the waitress said, "You're good sir. The gentleman in the corner paid for the drinks."

Cody turned to the man, he waved then looked away.

"Who's that?" Cody said.

"I don't know. It's too dark."

Cody stood and walked to the man's table to thank him. When he got to the table, he was surprised to see Eric.

"Eric," Cody said. "Thanks for the drink."

"I hope there are no hard feelings, Cody. Sometimes I run my mouth a little too much. I didn't know anything had happened to Karen."

Cody stood there deciding whether to accept his apology or not. The alcohol decided he would.

"Would you care to join us?" Cody said.

"Sure, if you don't mind," Eric said.

Cody walked Eric back to his table. "I hope you don't mind if Eric joins us," Cody said to Olivia.

"Not at all. Just promise me you won't hit him."

"We're okay," he said.

"How are you tonight, Olivia?" Eric said.

"Just havin' some fun. Do you want to dance?"

"Sure, I guess. I'm not promising you'll enjoy it," Eric said.

The two of them went to the dance floor. Just as they started to shake a little, the song was over and a slow song started. Eric put his arms around Olivia immediately and she slid into his embrace.

"How's he feeling?" Eric whispered.

"He's almost ready. When we get back to the table I'll get him to dance and you can put the powder in his drink."

"Sounds good to me. I'll be glad when this is over," Eric said.

"It won't be long. What about Cam?"

"He wasn't there. We'll call him when it's time. He'll come as fast as he can to save Diane. I'll get her tonight."

"Is Shaun secured?"

"Yep, I checked on him earlier. He's still tied up in the apartment. I don't think he'll ever wake up again."

"Okay, let's do this."

They broke the embrace and went back to the table. Olivia reached out to Cody.

"Come on and dance with me before this song is over," she said.

Cody got to his feet and went to the dance floor with Olivia. If he had to dance, it would be better with a slow song.

When the song finished they returned to the table. Eric nodded at Olivia. He had put the powder in his drink.

"Drink up," Eric said. "I have another bar I want to take you to. It's just a block away."

They finished their drinks and left together. No one paid any attention to the two helping the other out the door.

Chapter 37

I left the boat and drove to the hotel. I didn't have any luck there again. No one had seen them.

As I was standing in the lobby, my cell rang. It was Sly's number that appeared on the screen.

"Sly," I said.

"Cam, I think I found the man you were looking for."

"Really," I said, "That's good work since I never told you his name."

"You said a friend. I found a friend."

"Where would you like to meet to deliver this friend?"

"I'll call you tomorrow night with a location."

"Why not now?"

"He's not quite ready to come home yet."

"The twenty-thousand is for a whole person in good health," I said.

"We might have to prorate some of that," he said and hung up.

That worried me. Were they going to carve Dave up a little before returning him or just kill him?

I'll have my vengeance if they harm him.

As I was leaving, I saw Emily pull into the parking lot. I waited for her to get out of her car and start inside.

"Emily!"

She turned and saw me. The look on her face was one of surprise and shock.

"Cam," she said. "You're okay."

She put her arms around me. She was genuinely worried about me.

"Why shouldn't I be?" I said.

She was quiet. I could tell she wanted to tell me everything but didn't know if she should.

"Emily Barron," I said.

She stepped back and looked at me.

"How'd you know?"

"FBI, local police, Kailey. Everyone knew but me."

"I'm sorry, Cam. I couldn't tell you. I was afraid you'd tell the police. I couldn't take the chance."

"I understand that," I said. "But now that it's out in the open, what are we going to do?"

"I don't know. I've been looking for you. I was worried someone might have taken you."

"Olivia and Eric?" I said.

"Eric?" she said puzzled.

"He's Olivia's husband. He's the one who's been helping her kill everyone and probably your brother."

Emily turned white. "I've been such a fool," she said.

"She had us all fooled. At least you were on the right track suspecting her."

"I lost her a while ago. I was following her but I lost her in the traffic. She had Cody with her," she said, urgency in her voice.

"Where'd you last see them?"

"Roosevelt and Highway 1."

"Okay, you don't have to worry about me. Let's go see if we can find her car."

"I'm sorry, Cam," she said and kissed me.

It felt good and I didn't want it to end but I wanted to be with Kailey even more.

We took my car and drove to the intersection where she had last seen Olivia.

"I think she turned that way," Emily said pointing north on Highway 1.

We turned and drove toward Stock Island. There was a lot of areas to cover. We'd be lucky to find them. After thirty minutes of driving up and down the streets of the island, we called it quits.

"They could be anywhere," I said. "This is just the first Key. They might be all the way to Marathon for all we know."

"I don't think so. They want all the murders to take place near the festival."

"Yeah, you're probably right but it's getting dark. We'll have to look again in the morning," I said.

"Do you want me to stay with you tonight?" she asked.

I thought about it. Though I know it would be nice, it would only be one night. I didn't want to take any more chances with Kailey.

"I don't think it would be a good idea," I said. "My girlfriend is in town from Aspen. We've been together for a while even though we don't really live close to each other."

"I understand, Cam. I'll only be here a few more days. I did enjoy the time we had together."

"So did I. We were good together."

"Yes we were," and she smiled.

I took her back to her car, kissed her good night and left.

I called the sheriff's office and then Leland and told them where Olivia was last seen and that Cody was with her. They both said they would do what they could. It didn't sound like I was going to get much help.

I called Diane and Jack to see if they were okay.

"We're good, Cam. Just watching a movie."

"Where are you?"

"My house," Diane said.

"I'd feel better if you would stay at Jack's tonight," I said.

"You're such a worrier," Diane said. "We'll see after the movie."

"Please think about it. There's no sense in testing fate."

"Okay, love ya."

"Love you too. Goodnight."

I gave up and returned home. Walter met me at the gate and walked with me to the boat.

"Night, Cam," Stacy called from her boat.

"Night, Stacy. Thanks."

"You're such a good watchdog," I said to Walter.

He smiled at me. I don't think he understood the sarcasm.

I stepped onto the boat and knew immediately that I wasn't alone. I could feel it, but even more than that, I could see Kailey sitting naked at my patio table drinking my Wild Turkey.

"Hi big boy," she said. "I took the chance you'd be coming home alone."

I just stared. I never got tired of looking at her naked.

"You going to join me?" she said.

"Just give me a second," I said. "I'm not finished looking."

She laughed. "Get your clothes off," she said, "and I'll fix you a drink."

She stood and walked to the bar. I removed my clothes.

We spent the next two hours in an embrace under the stars. We made love then would have a drink, a snack and make love again. Life is good.

Finally, Kailey said she had to go. There was something she needed to do.

"What is it?" I asked.

"I'll tell you tomorrow," she said.

I walked her down the dock. She turned and kissed me long and tender.

"I love you, Cam and I always will," she said softly.

"I love you too, Kailey."

"Goodbye," she said, turned and walked away.

That sounded way too final. I wanted to follow her but I knew I shouldn't.

I returned to the boat, changed clothes and strapped my gun on. I needed to go to the Chastain home.

Chapter 38

The Chastain home was located a few blocks off Flagler on the west end of the island. Most locals knew where it was and chose to avoid it.

Thirty years ago it was a rundown, conch style, frame home. Now, due to the unlimited resources, the family has gained, the house is an enormous showplace. It's bordered front and rear by canals. There's a large swimming pool behind the house. It's been the center of many parties for the rich and famous of Key West.

It was as close to an impenetrable fortress as could be found on the island. All of which made my mission close to impossible.

It was midnight now. Maybe the security would be a little slack. I drove down the street in front of the house just to check out the security. I've been in the house a few times, so I knew the layout. If they were holding Dave here, I might not be able to save him.

The drive-by revealed two men standing inside the iron gate at the end of the driveway. They watched me as I passed. The worst part is now I have to turn around at the end of the street and drive back past the house. There's only one way in and one way out.

This time as I drove by, the gate was open, and one of the men was standing near the curb. He watched as I passed.

Crap, that's not good.

I drove back down to Flagler Street and parked along the curb. If I were going to gain access, it would have to be on foot.

I saw headlights coming off the street where the Chastain house was located. They were coming my way. I ducked down in the seat.

I heard the car pass and raised my head enough to watch which way they turned. I recognized the car as Sly's. He was heading west toward Highway 1. I decided to follow.

I stayed far enough back that he wouldn't notice me but close enough to keep eyeballs on.

He turned on 1 and drove north to Stock Island then turned right into the residential area. When he turned left onto Eighth Avenue I drove straight. I went one block to Ninth turned left and drove to the end of the street. I turned left again, went back to Eighth, and turned left. I was now coming up Eighth from the opposite direction. I could see the lights of his car in the driveway of a small house on the right. As I pulled to the curb, the car lights went off. The timer had expired, meaning he was already inside.

I parked and killed my lights so they wouldn't give me away. I walked to the house, taking note of the neighbors. All the houses were dark.

Moving between the house and the one next to it, I could see a light on in what I assumed was a back bedroom.

The blinds were closed but not tight. They were old and left a small slit between yellowed slats.

I put my face to the window and looked in. I could see Dave tied to a bed and Sly standing over him talking. I couldn't hear what he was saying but he didn't look happy.

Dave was shaking his head from side to side in a "No" motion. He had a gag in his mouth and blood was caked around his eye and mouth from a previous beating. That's when I noticed the blackjack in Sly's hand. It was a deadly instrument. Usually, one hit in the head and life was over.

I had to do something fast or Dave would be dead. I ran to the front door and knocked then ran around the house to the back door. It was a kid's game but it worked. I waited twenty seconds and kicked the back door open hoping Sly went to investigate the front.

The door flew open and I entered into the kitchen in a low stance with my gun held out in front of me. Dave was in the bedroom to my right and I could hear Sly running down the hallway toward me. I ducked down behind the refrigerator and waited.

The footsteps stopped. There was silence.

"Cam!" Sly said.

"Yep."

"What the hell do you think you're doing?"

"I came to get my friend. Thanks for finding him."

"Do you think I'm going to let you have him?"

"I was hoping so."

"I'm afraid the family overruled me on this one. He needs to be made an example of."

"I can't let you do that, Sly."

I heard a floorboard squeak in the hall and braced myself. Then as if an explosion went off Sly was in the kitchen rapidly firing his gun in every direction. I already had my gun trained on the entrance and took two quick shots. They both caught Sly in the chest.

He dropped his gun and fell to the floor. Blood was puddling around his torso.

He looked at me as I stood over him. Smiling he said, "Cam, the family's going to kill you for this."

He stared at the ceiling and I could see his eyes glaze over. He was dead.

I went into the bedroom and removed the gag from Dave's mouth.

"Cam," he said breathlessly. "How'd you find me?"

"Wanda," I said. "And I probably shouldn't have bothered."

"I'm sorry, man. I needed the money. I had to do something."

"So, you lost fifteen-thousand dollars to a mobster and then ripped his brother off to try to pay him back."

"When you put it like that..."

"Christ, Dave. Now they're going to kill me."

"Sorry, Cam."

I untied him and called the Key West PD. Sergeant Jackson answered. I told him what happened and gave him the address.

"What can you tell me about how they got you and what they said?" I asked Dave.

"They said they were going to cut me up some and then make me pay them double. I told them I couldn't even pay what I owed much less double."

"Great move, Dave."

"Then they said they would keep me locked up with the others in their private jail until I died."

"Others?" I said.

"Yeah, I guess they have other people locked up too. Anyway, when he came in this time he said there wasn't room for me so he was going to just kill me now and feed me to the gators."

"Did he say where the others were locked up?"

"No, just in their private jail."

Fifteen minutes later an ambulance arrived along with two city police cruisers and three sheriff cars.

Jackson had called Leland and got him out of bed. He didn't look very happy.

"Good morning, Cam," Leland said a little sarcastically.

"Chief," I said.

"What did you do now?"

"I killed Sly Chastain," I said.

The chief put his hand over his eyes and shook his head.

"Tell me the family doesn't know yet," he said.

"Not yet, but they will soon."

"What happened?"

I explained about Dave, who just stood there silently with blood all over his face.

"And that's not all," I said.

"There's more?"

"Dave told me that Sly insinuated they had others locked up in their private jail."

"Private jail?"

"Yeah, I think we need to move fast and raid the house. If any of this gets out they'll move them or kill them and dump the bodies in the swamps."

"Shit, Cam. Do you know what we're up against?"

"Yes I do, but it has to be done."

"We can't just raid Chastain's house because this little druggie says so," he said pointing at Dave.

"If we don't raid now, they'll have time to move the prisoners."

"I'm gonna call the S.W.A.T. team," Sheriff Rogers said.

"Yeah, okay you're right. Fuck!" Leland said.

Leland and the sheriff huddled in the corner. The sheriff made a call.

"We're getting a swat team formed to raid the Chastain house," Leland said. "Just having Dave held prisoner is enough to justify it but we better find some more prisoners."

"That's what they said," Dave said. "In their private jail. I told you when I called you that they were going to kill me."

"I don't know what you're talking about," Leland said and excused himself stepping into the backyard to make a call.

The coroner had the body removed and the medics were working on Dave. He was lucky to only have a few cuts and two black eyes.

"I'll take him back home if you're finished with him," I told Leland when he returned.

"For now, but don't you dare leave town," he said pointing a finger at Dave.

"Yes sir, I won't," Dave said.

I returned Dave to Wanda's house. Wanda was sitting on the front porch and when she saw us pull into the driveway, she ran to the car. She was in camouflage shorts and a tank top. This was pretty standard for Wanda.

"Go to bed, Dave. Don't go anywhere tonight," I said.

Wanda hugged me and kissed me numerous times on the cheek. I finally pushed her away.

"Both of you go in now and keep the doors locked," I said.

"Thanks, Cam. I owe ya, bro," Dave said again.

I backed out of the driveway and drove toward the Chastain house.

Chapter 39

Kailey slipped the gun under her pillow, pulled back the sheets and climbed into bed. She was more tired than she thought but her nerves were alive with anticipation. She looked at the clock beside the bed. One-fifteen a.m.

She worried about Cam and Diane. Where were they now and were they safe? Time will tell. By morning it should be over one way or the other.

She closed her eyes to rest. She would need all her strength for later.

Eric entered Diane's house through the back door using the key Olivia had made for him. It was well after midnight now, Diane should be asleep.

Eric moved down the hallway toward the bedroom where Diane slept according to Olivia. He bumped a table in the hall nearly causing a lamp to topple to the floor. He stood still for a full minute before moving on down the hall.

The door to Diane's room was ajar but mostly closed. He hoped the hinges were well oiled. Pushing the door open slowly he was glad to hear they were.

He could see a figure lying on the bed. In the pale moonlight slipping through the window, he could tell it was a woman with blonde hair. It was Diane.

He removed the cap on the bottle of ether and soaked the rag. The smell of the ether was strong. He wished he could hold it to his own nose and sleep the rest of the night. Now wasn't the time though. He had a job to do. It would be the last piece of the puzzle before the book was published and Olivia would be a bestselling author.

Eric slipped into the room and stood next to the bed. He would rather just climb into the bed with Diane. He could imagine how good it would feel. Instead, he lowered the rag to her nose and mouth. She jumped but settled back down quickly. She was out now.

He lifted her, carried her out of the house and placed her in the back seat of his rental car. She was wearing a t-shirt for pajamas. He pulled it up and looked at her body. *Very nice.*

Eric drove to the house he and Olivia had rented a month ago and prepared for this day.

He placed Diane on the bed and tied her hands to the headboard. Olivia would be there in an hour. He held the rag over her mouth again for ten seconds. That would keep her passed out for another hour. He pulled her t-shirt up over her head and removed her panties.

Just as he was climbing on top of her, he heard the front door open. *Shit.*

Olivia walked into the bedroom before he had time to dress.

"What the hell?" she yelled at him.

"I didn't do anything to her," he said.

"You would have if I hadn't come in."

"So, big deal, she'll be dead before the day is over."

"You're my husband, asshole. You're not supposed to be screwing other people."

"Yeah, like you and Cody?"

"That was business and he's as good as dead," she spat.

"Only because I'm going to kill him," he said. "You would never have done it."

"Let's put her clothes back on her and you stay away from her," Olivia said.

She picked up her panties, slipped them back on her, and then pulled her t-shirt down revealing her face.

"What the fuck!" she said. "What's she doing here?"

"It's Diane!" he said.

"No it isn't, that's Kailey, Cam's girlfriend."

Olivia reached down and pulled the blonde wig off Kailey.

"She was in Diane's bed," he said defensively. "I've never seen Diane before."

"Son of a bitch," she said. "What are we going to do now? It's supposed to look like Cody did this. They would know that he didn't get the wrong girl."

"Well, you're going to have to change the last chapter of your book. No big fuckin' deal."

"I don't like it," she said. "How'd she know we were coming for Diane and why'd she change places with her?"

"I don't know, but it'll work out just fine. Where's Cody?"

"I left him in the apartment. We'll bring him here when the time comes. I couldn't handle him by myself."

Eric looked at his watch. "We have two hours. Let's tape her to the metal chair and activate the timer on the bombs. I'll run the hot wire from the windows and doors to the timer. If anyone enters, the bomb will go off in fifteen seconds. Then we need to get to the truck and get Shaun ready for his ride.

"I don't like it," Olivia said.

"Do you want to be a bestseller or not?" Eric asked.

Olivia thought about it.

"Let's do it," she said.

Chapter 40

I parked on Flagler Street behind two squad cars. Sergeant Jackson was standing next to the cars on his cell phone. He hung up as I approached.

"The swat team is around the corner waiting for orders to rush the house," he said. "Leland told me to keep you here until the first wave was over."

"That's fine with me. I've had enough action for one night."

I decided to walk down to the canal where I could get a good view of the back of the house. From here, I could see the dock and several boats in their slips.

I started to turn and go back around front, when I saw a man running to one of the boats. He jumped in and released the lines.

The engine came to life and the boat away from the dock, turning in my direction.

He was coming toward me now, the front of his boat rising as the prop dug in the water. He saw me standing at the edge of the canal, raised his gun and fired. I heard the bullet hit a tree five feet from me.

I pulled my gun and fired two shots, both going wide and doing no harm. The driver and I made eye contact when he passed me. A look of recognition in his eyes as was in mine.

Olan Chastain.

As he passed, he raised his empty hand, finger pointing at me with his thumb up, he pulled the imaginary trigger and winked, then he was gone.

Shit!

I walked back to Jackson who was on his cell again. He hung up.

"Chastain got away," I said.

Jackson's radio sounded. "Clear to engage."

We heard the engines roar to life and watched as two armored trucks followed by six squad cars turned the corner and bolt down the street toward Chastain's house.

The next sound was a loud crash as the first truck rammed the gate. A flurry of gunshots was heard followed by a barrage of return fire. They were waiting for the raid. We could hear men shouting orders and the truck strike a solid surface.

"Sounds like they drove right into the house," I said.

"They did," he said. "That was the strategy."

"Are we going in?"

"No, we're staying right here to control the traffic. It wouldn't do any good to have an innocent bystander drive up on the scene."

It looked as if a war was taking place, and it was. I could see one armored truck at the gate blocking any escape and the other half was through the front door of the house.

An hour later, I met Leland at the gate of the estate.

"We got Charlie and five of their men, Olan got away," Leland said.

"Yeah, I saw him on the canal. I took a shot but missed. Worse yet, he saw me."

"He'll be too busy running to come after you," he said.

"Not after he finds out I killed his brother and busted his house. By the way, did you find anything?"

"Twelve prisoners. All girls from thirteen to twenty. He was running a sex slave op."

"Are they alright?"

"These are. They said they've only been here for three days, but they weren't the first. I guess he sold the last batch to make room for this one."

I felt sick. How could someone do that? The first man I killed, when I was seventeen, was doing the same thing with his own daughter.

"He won't be doing it again. He just lost everything. We'll find him," Leland said.

"He has the money to go anywhere in the world and the connections to get there," I said. "If he's not found in forty-eight hours, he won't be found."

"Well, we'll do what we can," he said. "Thanks for the lead on this. It was big."

"That's alright. I just wish it would have been a couple of years earlier."

"It could have been a couple of years later," he said. "I think we did well getting him when we did."

Chapter 41

Emily waited in her car one block from the garage apartment where she had followed Olivia. The lights were off and she hadn't seen any sign of life. There was a car parked at the curb in front of the house.

She had told Cam she lost Olivia in the traffic, but in truth, she wanted her to herself. If she decides to kill Olivia now, there would be no witnesses and Cam would say we didn't know where she was.

Now she knew Olivia was responsible for her brother and his family's deaths. She murdered all of them and made it look like Tom did it. She was going to pay for that. Olivia decided to walk around the garage and see if she could see in any windows.

It was dark here other than a little glow from the moon and Emily could take advantage of it. She crept along the bushes that lined the driveway until she reached the garage. The apartment was upstairs over the garage. A wooden stairway led to the front door.

Wondering if that was the only entrance, she moved to the rear of the garage. There was another stairway. It was more narrow and was probably only placed there for code.

Emily slowly climbed the stairs trying to levitate to decrease the noise the wooden steps made from her weight. When she reached the top, she stopped on the three-foot-square stoop. The door had a window but with the lights off inside and the curtain pulled, there was no way to see in.

What the hell. She examined the door more closely. It didn't look strong and there was a slight gap between the door and the jam. She ran back down the steps and checked the garage door with her cell phone light. The side door was unlocked. She opened it and entered.

It was dark in here but with her light, she could see well enough. She found what she was looking for immediately. A crowbar was leaning against the wall only two feet from the door. She grabbed it and ran back up the steps. She wanted to get in and out before Olivia returned.

Placing the crowbar between the door and the jam, it didn't take much pressure before the door popped open.

She stood back and to the side for a full minute before peeking through the open door.

It was still dark in the closed-up room but some moonlight filtered through the door.

The furniture was old and musty smelling. The place didn't look like it had been lived in for a long while.

As far as she could tell, there was a kitchen living/bedroom and a bathroom. She walked through the kitchen into the living room. The sofa was old and sagged in the center. Above the sofa was a window. She didn't want to turn on any lights in case Olivia returned. She would like to see better but if she opened the blinds that too would be a giveaway that someone was here.

She started when she heard a mumbled noise behind her. She spun around. Against the wall behind her, she could see two shapes.

"Hello," she whispered.

Moaning again.

Emily pulled the string on the window blinds and the room lit slightly from the front porch light.

Sitting in front of her and tied to their chairs was Cody and Shaun. Both men looked unconscious but Cody moved a little and groaned again.

"Cody!" Emily said.

She pulled the duct tape from his mouth and then Shaun's. Shaun still didn't move.

She patted Cody lightly on his cheek hoping to wake him. He stirred but was not going to wake.

She heard a car turning into the driveway and quickly pulled the string to close the blinds. She hoped she did it in time.

She took a chance and peeking out the slit in the blinds, she could see the car in the driveway. The doors opened and Olivia and Eric stepped out of the car.

Emily replaced the tape over the men's mouths and ran to the back door. She stepped out onto the landing, pulled the door shut and ducked down just as the front door opened.

"Hi guys, we're back," Eric said jovially.

"Enough," Olivia said. "Let's get them downstairs and into the car."

"When we get them settled in I want you to wait for thirty minutes before you come to the house," Eric said. "We'll plant Cody's body there next to Kailey's before the explosion and leave. Then we'll chain Shaun to the truck. We should be gone before either event occurs. It's two o'clock now. That'll give us a half hour to get out. We'll only need ten minutes."

Kailey? What are they doing with her? Emily could hear them lifting the men and carrying them out the front door one at a time. She took the opportunity to descend the staircase and sneak around the side of the garage. She saw them place Cody in the front seat and Shaun lying down in the back seat.

Eric kissed Olivia and said, "Thirty minutes."

He got in the car parked on the street and left. Olivia returned to the apartment.

Emily went back around the garage and climbed the stairs again. Peaking in the window, she couldn't see Olivia but the light in the bathroom was on.

She eased the door open, grabbed the crowbar she had left next to the door and stepped in.

She waited next to the bathroom door. When Olivia opened the door and stepped out Emily swung the crowbar low and Olivia's legs were knocked from under her. She hit the floor with a painful scream.

Emily could tell that Olivia's leg was broken. It had an irregular twist at the knee and blood was starting to run down her calf.

"God Damn, you bitch! What the fuck!" Olivia screamed in agony.

"This is what the fuck," Emily said and punched her in the jaw.

Olivia fell down on her side now. Emily grabbed Olivia's foot and twisted it. Olivia screeched in pain again.

"Stop, please stop," Olivia sobbed.

"You fucking cunt," Emily spat. "You killed my brother and his family just so you could write a book."

"Your Brother?

"Yes, Tom Barren," Emily said.

"Tom's your brother?"

"Yes, and now you're killing again for another book," she said and raised the crowbar.

"No, no, it wasn't me. It was Eric. I didn't even know he was going to do it."

Emily twisted her leg again and Olivia cried out in pain, louder this time.

"You had the fucking book written before he was even dead," Emily said and punched Olivia in the stomach.

"Please stop!" Olivia cried.

"Do you have Diane?"

"No, I haven't seen her."

"Where's Kailey?" Emily yelled in Olivia's face.

"I don't know what you're talking about," she panted.

Emily raised the crowbar over her head and looked at Olivia's other leg.

"No, no, please no!" Olivia cried. "I'll tell you."

Emily lowered the crowbar.

"Where is she?" she shouted.

"Cow Key. It's an old house sitting off to the right of the road on 5th Street."

"What's the address?"

"There is none," Olivia cried grabbing her knee as new pain shot its way up her leg. "It's the only house there. Past the barricades and down the path."

Emily retrieved the rope from the chair where Cody had been tied and bound Olivia's hands behind her. She then tied her feet together, causing more pain in her leg. After connecting the two behind Olivia, she stood.

"Please, you have to call an ambulance for me. My leg is broken."

233

"Later maybe," Emily said. "First I'm going to call Cam so he can get Kailey before the house blows. If you gave me bad information, I'll be back here to break your other leg and both elbows."

"It's true, it's true," she said in a panic.

"How long before the bomb explodes?"

"Three o'clock," Olivia cried.

Emily looked at her watch. "A half-hour."

"No, it's only two now," Olivia said. "You have an hour."

"No, it's two-thirty. I heard Eric tell you to come in a half hour. I think he was planning on you being there when the bomb went off," Emily laughed.

"That son of a bitch," Olivia said. "He was going to claim the book for himself."

"And I bet there was going to be a special chapter in the end how Cody took his girlfriend with him when he died," Emily said smiling.

Emily pulled her cell phone out and called Cam as she ran to Olivia's car.

Chapter 42

My cell rang. It was Emily.

"What are you doing up so late?" I answered.

"I don't have time to explain. You have twenty-five minutes to get Kailey out of the house."

"Kailey?"

"Yeah, they took her instead of Diane."

"Where?" I asked.

She gave me directions. I had just left the Chastain house and turned toward Highway 1.

I knew the area and figured it would take around ten minutes to get there this time of night. I was on Highway 1 in record time but now there were two cars driving side by side in front of me. We were coming up on a business area on Stock Island. I took a chance and passed on the right using a parking lot. I pulled back out barely missing a car and almost missed my turn on McDonald Avenue.

I took the shortcut and was on 5th Street in one block. At the end of the street, there was a barricade. I blew through it scraping the side of my car and knocking my mirror off. The road was sandy and I fought for traction. Close to the end of the path, I saw an overgrown trail which I didn't know was there. I hoped I had the right place.

I stopped the car and ran down the trail. I could see the roof of a house in the moonlight peeking through the clouds as I tore through the mangrove trees and finally stepped into a small clearing.

~***~

Eric sat in his car in the QuickStop parking lot at Highway 1 waiting for Olivia to drive by to her death. He didn't see Cam turn a block early and take the shorter route to 5th Street.

~***~

The house was run down. The paint was chipping and some of the shingles were missing. It was sitting on a block foundation. That was a little unusual, but not unheard of for the keys. Usually, the home would be on stilts to keep it dry. There was evidence of flooding to the exterior of the house. It was dark inside and I couldn't tell if Kailey was in there or not.

I knew if I entered the house, it would erupt in fire and I'd never be able to get Kailey out. I hoped I could save her, but time was short. If I had the wrong house, then Kailey would die. The stage was already set. There was no turning back even for Olivia and Eric. They would never publish the final chapter of this book if I could help it.

I knew from Cody's book that they had rigged the doors and windows to explode fifteen seconds after one of them was opened. I didn't see any skylights or attic access. I was also aware that the clock was ticking and I only had about ten minutes to get her out before the house would explode on its own.

There was a garage behind the house. I ran to it in desperation trying to find something that would be useful. The side door had a padlock secured through a hasp. I lowered my shoulder and hit the door with all my strength. It gave away to a shower of splinters.

I reached for the light switch and then thought better of it. What if it was on the same circuit as the house? It might set off the bomb.

I pulled my cell phone from my pocket to turn on the flashlight. I paused briefly to look at the time. I had twelve minutes left. I shone the light around the garage. There was a workbench with screwdrivers and pliers hanging above it. There were three large cabinets along one wall. I opened them one at a time.

~***~

Inside the house, Kailey sat in the metal chair watching the red numbers on the timer countdown.

She had quit pulling at the restraints realizing it was futile to try to escape.

She thought about how much she was in love with Cam, and that she would never see him again. This made her even sadder than the fact that she was going to die in–she looked at the timer–six minutes.

I hope Cam finds Olivia and Eric and I hope he doesn't find me. If he enters this house, he'll die with me. If I could just live long enough to tell him how much I really do love him then I wouldn't mind so much if I did die.

Kailey glanced at the timer again. Four minutes. Tears started to form in her eyes. She didn't realize how precious life was to her. She was glad she saved Diane. She knew Cam would never be able to cope with losing her. Diane was Cam's reason for living now.

She thought about the first time she met Cam. *She walked into her library and found him standing there with her soon to be son-in-law. Cam had a beautiful smile that made her*....she couldn't think anymore. What was that noise that was intruding on her final thoughts?

It was getting louder, then thunderous. Light broke through the wall across the room from her chair. The noise grew in intensity and the light filled the room.

The sound finally died out and Cam stuck his head through the hole he had cut in the side of the house. He shined his flashlight around.

"Kailey!" I yelled.

"Go away Cam, there isn't time. I love you but please run!" Kailey yelled back.

I stepped back and picked up the chainsaw again. I started it and cut the hole in the wall big enough to get through and then a little more.

I threw the saw to the ground, rolled through the opening and ran to Kailey. I didn't have time to free her so I picked her up, chair and all and ran for the opening. I jumped through turned grabbed the chair with Kailey in it and pulled her through. The house shook with small explosions that traveled around the exterior walls, setting off flames as it went. We were thrown to the ground. I regained my footing, lifted Kailey and ran another fifty feet before falling to the ground. We were safe.

She lay on her side facing me. We smiled at each other and kissed. That's when she jerked and blood sprayed my face. She had been shot.

I pulled her behind a tree, opened my pocketknife and cut her lose. Her shoulder was bleeding badly.

I pulled my gun from the back of my belt and snuck a look around the tree. My reward was a bullet that sprayed bark into my eyes. Everything was blurry and I could feel blood running down my face.

I heard footsteps in the gravel driveway, but I couldn't see.

I reached around the tree and fired blindly in the direction of the footsteps. I heard a man yell in pain. The footfalls retreated at a run.

"Kailey," I said, "are you okay?"

"Yes," she whispered.

"I'll call an ambulance."

I ripped off my shirt and applied pressure to Kailey's wound.

"You'll be okay. It looks like the bullet went straight through."

I heard another car stop on the road at the top of the path.

I pulled my gun. "Kailey, can you see who's coming down the path?" I said and pointed my gun in that direction.

"Don't shoot," Kailey said. "It's Emily."

Emily ran to us and bent down over Kailey.

"How did you know where Kailey was?" I asked.

"Olivia told me. It seems she has a low pain threshold. We were right about her writing the book. It was called, Murder Fest Key West," Emily said.

"Who was the bad guy?" I asked.

"It was going to be Cody. He's okay," Emily said.

I could hear the ambulance coming.

"Hang in there Kailey," I said.

"I'm fine," she said in a weak voice. "I love you."

"I love you too."

She smiled, "I told ya, you would someday."

"I have for a long time."

"Thanks, Emily," Kailey whispered then closed her eyes and faded away.

Chapter 43

Eric, hiding in the scrub trees along the lane, watched as Cam and Emily attended to Kailey. He felt his own wound, his hand coming away sticky. *Shit.*

He half crouched and returned to his car. He was going to need help with his gunshot. He needed to find Olivia.

The ambulance arrived followed by two firetrucks, a police cruiser, and two sheriff cars. Everyone else was still tying up loose ends at the Chastain house.

The EMT's worked on Kailey then loaded her in the ambulance.

Emily drove me to the hospital.

"So, you were right all along. Olivia killed your brother and his family, just to write a book," I said.

"And now she's killed all these people in Key West with the help of Eric. I can't believe that creep's her husband."

"Where's Cody and Shaun?"

"I left them in Olivia's car. They're going to be okay."

"And Olivia?"

241

"She's a little tied up. She broke her leg."

"Good."

"Where did Eric go?"

"I don't know. I think he was going to blow Olivia up with Cody in the house."

"Really?"

"Yep, I believe he was going to steal the book."

At the hospital, they flushed my eyes and a few minutes later, I was back to eighty percent.

I checked on Kailey. The doctor said she was lucky. The bullet passed through without hitting any vital organs or vessels. She'd be sore for a few weeks but she'd recover fully.

I called Leland to fill him in.

"What the hell, Cam. Is this all you can manage to tear up in one night?"

"Not my fault. Too many bad people out there."

"You're like a fucking magnet when it comes to bad people."

I ignored his sarcasm.

"Did you get Cody and Shaun?"

"There's a car there now. They said they were fine, other than being all drugged up."

"What about Olivia?"

"She wasn't there."

"Emily said she left her tied up in the house with a broken leg."

"I guess she hobbled away. The ropes had been cut and were laying there. There was blood."

"Eric," I said. "He had to have gotten her."

"Probably so. She *is* his wife."

"Yeah, I know, but he was going to blow her up along with Cody and Kailey."

"Change of heart," Leland said, "but we'll get 'em. He's been shot and she has a broken leg. How fast can they be?"

"Any word on Olan?" I asked.

"Nothing."

There's too many loose ends. How did I get involved in all this? Emily and Dave. I need new friends.

Diane and Jack walked in. Now I was going to be in *real* trouble.

"Cam," Diane said hugging me. "Are you okay?"

"I'm fine sweetie."

"Thank you, Emily, for calling me," Diane said.

"I knew you'd want to be here."

"So, Olivia killed your brother and his family."

"That's right. I knew it had to be her. Moreover, I suspected she had a hand in the murders here. I was right about that too."

"Can we see Kailey?" Diane asked.

"Sure, go on in," I said pointing to her room.

Diane went in to see Kailey while Jack stayed with me.

"We have to find Olan," I said.

"Where was he last seen?"

"Pointing a gun at me on the canal behind his house. If I don't find him I'll be looking over my shoulder until they get me."

"Is that the worst mobster you could find to fuck over?"

"I don't know any others."

Emily told him about Olivia and Eric.

"At least Cody's safe. Are we going to hunt them too?" Jack asked me.

"Not me. I don't really care about them right now. The police can handle them."

"I can't believe you're going to let the police handle something for a change. You must be growing wise in your old age."

"Not really. I'm just fighting for my life now," I said.

"I'm going to hunt them," Emily said.

"I can't stop you, but I wish you wouldn't," I said.

"I have to."

"I can understand that. Just be careful."

Diane returned. "Cam, I want you to go home and get some rest. I want to stay here with Kailey tonight. She took my place to protect me and almost died in the process. I owe her, big time."

"I don't think I should leave her."

"You have to get some sleep. The doctor said she'll probably go home tomorrow. You'll need your strength."

I went in and checked on Kailey. She was sleeping. I kissed her and left. Diane sat in the reclining chair next to her bed and promised she would call me if anything changed.

I thanked Emily again and kissed her goodbye. Jack drove me back to the boat.

Chapter 44

Eric drove to Marathon Key before stopping at a motel. Olivia was in a lot of pain and was letting him know.

"Please, Eric," she cried. "Get me to a hospital."

"We can't, baby. The police have to be watching all the medical facilities. I'll fix your leg until we can find some help."

He watched the motel office for a minute before getting out of the car, zipping his jacket to hide the blood and walking in.

"Good morning," the lady behind the counter said. "Can I help you?"

Eric gave her his best smile and said, "Yes. My wife and I have been driving all night and would like a room for a few days.

Eric unlocked the motel room door and returned to the car to help Olivia. He ended up carrying her to the room.

Once settled into the bed Olivia said, "You son of a bitch. Emily said you were going to kill me along with Cody."

Eric looked at her amused. "She was trying to get in your head," he said. "I would never harm you and you know it. That's why I came back for you. We're going to get out of this mess and write that book. We might have to change a few things and sell it on the black market now but we'll still make millions."

He was talking ridiculous. They would never be able to release that book. It would hang them.

"I love you, baby," he said. "We're good."

She regarded him suspiciously. He was lying. She could tell. He just needs someone to help him with his gunshot, and then she'd be of no use to him.

He removed his jacket revealing a blood-soaked shirt. He gingerly pulled the shirt off. There was a hole in his right side and blood was seeping out slowly. He turned away from Olivia and asked, "Did it go through?"

She looked at his back. There was a neat hole there also but it was three inches lower than the entry hole.

"Yeah, it came out but it did some traveling while it was in there," she said.

He sat on the edge of the bed and put his head in his hands.

"I've got to find us some help," he said. "Take off your blouse."

"What for?"

"I want you to wrap my wound as tight as you can so I can go find us a doctor."

"You'll never make it, Eric. They'll be watching."

"I'll find a way. I can at least get us some bandages and a splint for your leg."

She removed her blouse and wrapped it around his midsection. She tied the arms in a knot and pulled it as tight as she could. He winced from the pain.

After he caught his breath, he put his gun in his waistband and pulled his jacket back on. Opening the door he said, "I'll be back in an hour."

~***~

Stacy's boat was dark. I figured she and Barbie were at Coyote Ugly, but it was awfully late. Then I realized it wasn't late at all. It was early morning. They were still sleeping.

I heard a dog bark. Walter was lying on the front patio of Stacy's boat. He ran to me.

"What are you doing out here again, boy?"

He wouldn't say but he didn't look happy about it.

"Come on, let's get you some water and food."

He walked beside me until we arrived at the boat then he moved in front of me and blocked my entrance.

"You have to get out of the way if you want to go in," I said.

The hair stood up on his back and he stared at the boat's door. I could hear a deep growl coming from his throat.

"What is it, Walter?"

He lunged at the door barking and growling furiously, pawing the glass. I've never heard him sound so ferocious. He'd keep me away.

I pulled my gun and moved to the door. I stood beside it and opened it swinging my gun in first. Walter tore through the opening and bolted across the living room.

I heard a man scream and the door to the side deck slam. Walter was at the door still barking.

"Get back Walter," I said.

He did. I opened the door and pointed my gun again. I heard a splash and ran to the railing. I could see a man swimming away from the boat. I aimed but didn't pull the trigger. I didn't know who it was and didn't want to shoot a kid who might have been just stealing anything he could find.

My little voice in my head told me I'd barely escaped being murdered. It had to be Olan or one of his thugs.

I bent down and petted Walter. "Thanks, boy. I owe you another trip to the doggie bar."

He licked me.

But now seeing Walter reminded me about Dave. I need to tell him what has happened. His life will be in danger too.

I called his cell and got no answer. That didn't surprise me. Just the same, I felt I should go find him.

I fed Walter and gave him a treat. He laid it in his bowl with his food. I think he was too wound up to eat.

When I opened the door to leave Walter made his escape once more. I reckoned he was going with me again.

When we got in the car, I called Leland to tell him about the intruder.

"Shit, Cam. I wish I'd of never given you my number."

"Then you'd never solve any crimes," I said jokingly.

"I'll have a car patrol the area," he said.

"I doubt if he'll be back but maybe you can search this part of town. I'm going to Dave's to make sure he's okay."

"If you're going to check on him then *you'll* have to go there alone. We don't have any free cars."

"I figured as much. Get some sleep and I'll talk to you tomorrow."

"Sleep? What's that?"

When I pulled into Wanda's driveway, the moon was disappearing and the sun was coming up. I could already feel the humidity in the air. Her car was in the drive.

I told Walter to stay in the car but I had the top down, so it was really up to him.

Shadows played on the front of the house from a Jamaican Dogwood tree that was moving in the breeze in the center of the yard. The low sun amplified the size of the tree and made shadows long and ominous.

I stepped onto the porch and immediately noticed the front door was ajar. This wasn't good. After inspecting it, I could see it had been forced violently. The frame was splintered and the security chain was dangling with a large portion of the door still held in place with the screws. Something or someone heavy had forced it.

As if sensing my fear, Walter jumped out of the car and ran to my side.

I eased the door open and stepped in.

"Dave! Wanda!" No answer.

I walked through the house searching from room to room. I found Wanda lying on the floor near the rear door.

Chapter 45

Feeling for a pulse, I detected one although it was weak. She had a stream of blood on her cheek. Upon inspection, I discovered a gash in the back of her head.

I could hear Walter moving from room to room. No doubt he picked up Dave's sent and was searching for him. After a thorough inspection, he finally returned to my side.

I called Leland and then an ambulance for the second time today.

Wanda didn't regain consciousness while we were still there. The EMT seemed to think she would live. It was evident what happened to Dave anyway. Someone grabbed him and escorted him to Olan.

"Is Wanda okay?" a voice from the doorway said.

I turned to see a man in his seventies standing there. He had his pajamas on and a ball cap with a grey ponytail hanging down his back.

"Who are you?" I asked.

"Taylor," he said. "I live next door." And pointed to the house on the left. "I heard all the commotion and then you arrived right after the car drove away."

"What car was that?"

"The black sedan that Dave got into with Ricco Romero."

The name struck a chord with me. He was one of Chastain's henchmen. Rumor has it, by reliable sources, that Ricco worked as a bodyguard for Eduardo Mendoza, head of the Mexican Nuevo Cartel, in Juarez for four years before migrating to Key West where he became an enforcer for Olan Chastain. We believe he was sent here to keep an eye on Chastain. The word is Ricco is only used when there are no other means of retaliation. They say if he touches you, you're as good as dead.

"You know Ricco?" I asked.

"Yep, I've had a few run-ins."

"Was Dave walking or being carried?"

"A little of both, I'd say. They don't let you walk much. Makes 'em feel tough."

"Do you know the make of the car?"

"Yeah, you got a pen and paper?"

"I can remember the make," I said.

"Can you remember the license plate?"

I got a paper from one of her kitchen drawers and a pencil then wrote down the tag number.

"Thanks. This will be a big help."

"Another car was parked down the street. It followed them as they left. Want the tag on that one?"

When Leland arrived, I gave him the info and introduced him to Taylor.

"Hey Tay," he said. "What are you doing here?"

"Helping you guys, 'cause I know you can't find your nose without help."

"Fuck you."

"You're welcome," Taylor said and smiled.

"I take it you two know each other," I said.

"We've had some run-ins," Leland said.

Police Patrolman, Dwaine Hopkins entered the room and handed Leland a cup of coffee and a McDonald's sack.

"Thought you might need this," he said.

Leland took a swig of the coffee and inspected the sack. He pulled out an Egg McMuffin and dropped the sack on the kitchen table.

"Which way did the guys go?" Leland asked.

"Down that way," he said pointing. "But you know, they could turn at the next street."

Leland just stared at him. "How'd you have time to get the tag number?"

"I copied it off the movie," he said grinning big enough to count all five teeth.

"Movie?"

"Yeah, wanna see it? I took it with my night vision camera when they were leaving."

Leland took a big bite of the sandwich and laid it on the sack. "Give me that," he barked.

We watched the movie. A big man, Ricco, was dragging Dave out of the house and into his car. Dave was trying to resist, but with his feet barely touching the ground, it was useless. There was the license plate. Then after they pulled out of the drive, a second car from a half block down pulled away from the curb and followed them. There were two men in that car. Taylor had zeroed in on that plate too.

"Can you send a copy of that to my phone?" Leland asked.

"What do I get?" Taylor said.

"I'll think of something," Leland said.

"Well, I guess there's a first time for everything."

Taylor zipped around his camera and Leland's phone beeped.

"There it is," Taylor said.

"Thank you. You coming over for supper Thursday?" Leland said.

"Wouldn't miss it," Taylor said.

"See ya then," Leland said.

"Anyway, I hope Wanda's okay," he said, tipped his hat and left.

"What was that?" I asked.

"My Uncle," Leland said. "My fucking Uncle."

Chapter 46

Leland ran the plates and, of course, they were registered to Surfside Limo Company that was owned by ProCar Leasing, which was owned by Trainer Automotive and so on. We weren't going to get an address on that vehicle.

The second car was registered to Angelo Perez.

"What the hell's he doing here?" Leland said.

"Who's he?" I asked.

"Cuban cartel out of Miami. They're some bad mothers. Why are they following Olan's men?"

"Maybe they're looking for Olan too. Do they work together?"

"Yeah, they have some dealings."

"My guess then is they're here to tie up loose ends."

"Maybe they're afraid Olan will talk if we get him," Leland said.

"You've got Charlie in jail don't you?"

"Yeah, we'll get him to talk. He never was too tough and he hates his brother. Rumor is, he's planning to off Olan and take over the family business."

Leland called the station to put an APB out on the two license plates.

"They're armed and dangerous," he said. "Don't take any chances."

"Where do *you* think Olan would go?" I asked.

"That's anybody's guess," he said. "We're going to check all the street cams. I'm sure he'll show up in one of them. They're everywhere."

"I wonder if we'll ever see Dave again?"

"What's wrong with him anyway?"

"Other than just plain stupidity you mean?"

"Yeah, other than that."

"Drugs and alcohol," I said. "But you know he hasn't done anything illegal. He sold some guy a bag of tea leaves. No law against that."

"Okay then, if we get him back I'm going to charge him for selling groceries without a license."

Leland picked up his sandwich and took another bite. He looked at it, "Not bad."

"What are you doing about Eric and Olivia?"

"We're looking. Checking all the medical offices, veterinarians and med schools in the Keys. There was quite a bit of blood in the apartment. You must have hit him pretty good."

Five minutes later Leland's phone rang.

"What? Son of a bitch," he said and hung up.

"What now?" I asked.

"They just found Charlie dead in his cell. He's been shot."

"How?"

Leland threw the remains of his cold sandwich against the wall, "I don't know. They have their ways."

Chapter 47

Eric looked up the Veterinarian's office address on his cell phone. They would open at eight o'clock. He had time to get there before they unlocked their doors.

The parking lot was empty so Eric backed into the first spot and waited.

Five minutes later a blue SUV pulled into the lot with a vanity plate that read, "DOGDOC".

A man in his sixties got out of the car at the same time Eric did. He greeted Eric as he walked past his car, "Good morning," he said, "I'll be open in about five minutes."

"Okay," Eric said but didn't back away from the door.

The doctor opened the door and stepped in. Eric was on his heels.

"Would you mind waiting outside until I get everything ready," the doctor said.

Eric pulled his gun out and pointed at the man. "Yes, I would," he said.

Eric closed the door behind him as the Doc backed across the room.

"I don't keep any money here," he said in a shaky voice.

"I don't need any money. I need you to get your supplies and come with me."

Eric opened his jacket and revealed his bandage.

"I've got a bullet wound I want you to repair and my wife has a broken leg. Get whatever it is you'll need for that and get in my car."

"I can't operate on you. I'm a Vet.," he said.

"You can and you will or I'll kill you and wait for your assistant."

Doctor Kenny didn't want that. His assistant is Melanie, his daughter.

He started throwing bandages and medicines into his bag and picked up a variety of splints. "I'll have to rig something up with these," he said, referring to the splints. "They're too small for humans."

"They'll be fine. She won't need 'em that long anyway. Let's go," he said motioning to the door.

Eric ordered the doctor to get in behind the wheel and drive. He gave him directions to the motel.

When they reached the room, Eric knocked once and opened the door. Olivia was lying on the bed, tears in her eyes. She looked at the doctor, fear, and alarm on her face.

"Who's that?" she said.

"Doctor Kenny," Eric said.

The Doctor nodded to Olivia and set his bag on the bed beside her.

"Me first," Eric said pointing the gun.

The Doctor did what he could to stop the bleeding and shot him up with an antibiotic.

"That's all I can do. You need to get to a hospital," he said.

"Fix her," Eric replied.

Olivia screamed when the Doc moved her leg. "Sorry," is all he said.

He fashioned a temporary splint out of three splints he had that were better formed for dogs.

"This won't help much but it's better than nothing," he said.

Eric's bleeding had stopped and the area was feeling better. Olivia was still in pain.

"Here are some pain pills for both of you," the Doc said. "Don't overdo them. They'll hold you until you can get real help."

The Doctor stood and started to put his supplies back into the bag.

"Have a seat, Doc. You're not going anywhere," Eric said.

"I have patients today. They need me at the clinic."

"They'll get along," he barked and pointed the gun at him.

The Doctor sat down in a dirty recliner next to the window. He knew there was no way he was going to be able to walk out of here. This was a desperate man. Whatever had happened to him, I'm sure he deserved.

Chapter 48

At eight o'clock that morning, after helping Kailey with breakfast, Diane went to the toxicology office to pick up the blood test. Cody had traces of Rohypnol in his blood along with ether.

My cell rang. It was Diane.

"Looks like we were right about Cody being drugged," Diane said.

"He was lucky to come out of this alive."

"Let's just hope it's over. Any word on them?"

"Nothing yet," I said and gave her the fifty cent tour of Dave's latest.

"When are you going to get some sleep?" she asked.

"I'm heading to the hospital now, then home. How's Kailey?"

"She's fine. We just finished breakfast. She'll probably go home with me today."

"That's not a good idea. Eric and Olivia are still on the loose and they have a score to settle. Bring her to my boat and both of you spend the day there. I'll call Jack and ask him to come over."

"If we do, will you go to bed for a while?"

"I promise."

"I'll see you in fifteen minutes. I want to check in on Cody while I'm there. Have you seen him?"

"I'm looking at him right now," she said. "He just walked in."

Diane stood and hugged Cody. "You want to talk to Cam?"

"Hey ya, Cam," he said taking the phone.

"Cody. Good to hear your voice. How are you feeling?"

"Couldn't be better. I'm in a room with the two most beautiful girls in Key West."

"I'll be there shortly," I said.

"Take your time, Cam."

I turned onto College Road toward The Lower Keys Medical Center.

I was tired. I haven't slept for twenty-six hours and it was starting to catch up with me. I think that was why I didn't notice the car pull out of Sunset Marina Road toward me and slow down as we approached one another.

The sun was coming up now and when I reached up to lower my visor, it was blown out of my hand. I could hear gunfire and the bullets were riddling my car. I felt a pain in my leg and knew I'd been hit. I lay down in the seat and pressed the accelerator to the floor. The gunfire was louder and intensified as I scraped along the side of the car the shots were coming from. Once past, I rose up again and looked back over my shoulder. The car was doing a power slide one-eighty and coming back at me.

I knew I didn't have a chance against the automatic weapons protruding from the windows of the black sedan so I punched the pedal again and flew into the med center parking lot.

My leg was stinging but I didn't have time to worry about it, I might be dead in less than a minute if I didn't handle the situation.

I pulled between two parked cars for protection, pulled my gun out and opened the door. That's when I noticed that Walter had been hit too. "Stay down boy," I said pushing him to the floorboard.

As soon as I got out of the car, the black sedan skidded to a stop fifty feet away. I opened fire the same time they did.

I felt another sting on my right shoulder but kept firing at the car. I saw one of the shooters fall back into the car as blood sprayed from the open hole in his forehead.

The driver accelerated and sped away, tires squealing.

I leaned against the car for a second until I was sure they were gone. "Walter, you okay, boy?"

I heard him moan and then a soft bark.

I managed to get to my feet and open the passenger door. Walter was still on the floorboard looking at me.

Now people were starting to ask how I was and a wheelchair appeared by my side.

Two doctors and a swarm of nurses were guiding me to the chair.

"I'm okay," I said. "Check on Walter."

They looked at each other and then the car.

"Walter," one of them said as he went back to the car.

"Give me some help over here!" I heard him yell.

I turned in the chair and saw them lifting Walter from the car. He looked at me as they carried him past.

"He'll be okay," the doctor said.

The nurse pushed me into the hospital while the other doctor checked my wounds.

"Looks like you're both lucky today," he said.

"I don't feel lucky," I said.

"It could have been a lot worse."

As they were wheeling me into the elevator, a hand reached around and held the door. It was Jack.

"Cam, what the hell?"

"My guess is Olan's men," I said.

"I was pulling onto College Road when a black Chevy came flying through the stop sign," Jack said. "They didn't make the turn and rolled over on the Highway. I'd heard the shots though, and came on in. I didn't know it was you."

"Call Leland and make sure those guys don't get away."

Jack pulled his phone out and dialed.

When he hung up, I asked him if he'd check on Walter.

He looked at the doctor. "Down the hall in same day surgery, I think," the doctor said. "Cam will be in emergency when you're done."

Jack left. "I'll be right back."

"Stay with him as long as you need to," I said.

I was sitting up in my bed being stuck with needles and having my clothes cut off when I saw Diane through the window. I guess Jack called her. I smiled and gave her a small wave. She had tears in her eyes, but she brightened a little at my gesture.

Jack appeared at her side and gave me a thumbs up. Walter was going to be okay.

The anesthesiologist came in the room and five minutes later, I was a goner.

When I woke, Kailey was sitting next to my bed in a wheelchair. She smiled and touched my hand.

"You couldn't let me be one up on you, could you?" she said.

She was wearing a blue sling to support her shoulder from her gunshot. I looked down at my arm– identical.

I smiled, "Steady slings," I said.

Diane and Jack were standing across the room talking to Leland.

"What are you whispering about over there?" I asked as loud as I could. They could barely hear me though.

"Don't exert yourself, Cam," Diane ordered.

I cocked my head and looked at Kailey. "She's right," she said.

I nodded and closed my eyes. The next time I woke Kailey was the only one in the room with me.

"Hey, sleepyhead," she said.

It made me smile.

"Did I get rid of them?"

"Yeah, they left about an hour ago."

"Did they get the guy who shot me?"

"Leland has the driver and one of the gunmen down at the station. The other gunman didn't make it."

"Who are they?"

"Olan's men."

A minute later I asked, "How's Walter?"

"Just a flesh wound. Cody took him back to the boat."

"Good. I was worried; he's not tough like me."

"Oh yea, he got shot and walked out of here. You're still lying around."

I noticed my leg was bandaged too. I had forgotten I was shot twice.

"How's my leg?"

"You'll walk with a cane for few weeks at the most."

"Will you marry me?"

"Yes, but not now. For one thing, you're all drugged up."

"And for another?" I asked.

"For another," she said. "I still have a way to go before I'm safe to be around."

"The day will come."

"It better."

I saw a police deputy standing outside the room.

"Guard?" I said shifting my eyes toward him.

"Leland said you needed him. I agreed."

I chuckled, "Christ, they just lost a prisoner in their own jail. They can't protect me from the cartel."

"We can try," she said.

"We?"

She raised the pillow on her lap and revealed a pistol. I never leave home without it," she said.

"Who brought that to you?"

"I have my people," she said blankly. "Someone's going to die for what they've done to you."

I didn't feel like arguing with her but I wouldn't let her go feeling this way.

The door opened and Emily walked in. She bent down and hugged Kailey. "How ya feeling?"

"Not bad," Kailey said. "Thanks again for your help."

"I don't deserve thanks. It's because of me that Cam got in this mess."

"Not true," I said. "Cody was a target. I was destined to get into this mess even if you weren't here. Besides, if you wouldn't have found Olivia and convinced her to tell me where Kailey was, she'd be dead now."

"Diane got the test result's back," Kailey said. "Cody had traces of Rohypnol in his system. Olivia was drugging him at the time of the murders and setting him up. My guess is she did the same to your brother."

"I should have killed that bitch while I had her," Emily said.

"She's not going to get away," I said. "A broken leg is a hard thing to hide."

"Yeah, maybe. Anyway, I wanted to tell the two of you goodbye. I'm going to search for Eric and Olivia. That journey might take me to the ends of the earth. I might not be back here."

"Have you settled things with Leland? I know he's going to want to go over all the details."

"The FBI has taken over the case. They said they'd be in touch."

"Figures, after Leland did all the work, they want the credit."

"I'll make sure the world knows who deserves the credit," Emily said.

She leaned over me and kissed me. I hoped Kailey wouldn't shoot her. Then she and Kailey kissed and Emily said goodbye. I watched her leave. Another chapter in my life is gone.

Chapter 49

An hour later Leland appeared in my room. I was alone.

"You look like shit," he said.

"I haven't been sleeping well."

"I brought you a present cause I felt sorry for you," he said dropping a white sack on the bed.

I looked at the sack, "Betty's?" I said.

He grinned. "Diane's suggestion."

"What's the latest?"

"On which case?"

"Pick one," I said.

"Okay, no sign of Olivia and Eric. The FBI has decided they can do a better job than I can on that one. It's only a matter of time before they take my Cartel case too. I'm surprised they haven't yet."

"Are Olan's men talking?"

"Not a word. They're closed up like a steel trap."

"So, what do you want from me? You're here for a reason other than to bring me a roll."

"I just came to warn you. They want you bad for killing Sly. Dave's probably already dead and I'm afraid you're next."

"And?"

Leland looked around the room. He didn't want to make eye contact with me.

"We have men watching you. If they come, we'll get them."

"So, are you going to tether me to a tree out in the hospital yard and wait for the wolves to come?"

"It's not like that, Cam. Your safety is our first concern."

"Like Charlie's?"

Leland skipped a beat then said, "Do you have your gun?"

I paused a minute then said, "That locker over there," and I nodded toward my closet.

"Do you think you need a gun, Cam?"

"Did Charlie have a gun?"

"No."

"Then let's do this one different."

Leland handed me my gun. I slid the rack back. No bullets in the chamber. I dropped the clip out. It was empty too. I looked at him. "I think I used all my ammo."

He reluctantly pulled a clip from his pocket and handed it to me.

"Glad to see we think alike," I said.

"I've never carried anything other than a nine millimeter."

I pushed the clip in and racked one into the chamber, then slid the gun under my sheet.

"The nurse is going to think you're happy to see her," he said.

"Have you seen her? You'd be happy too."

Leland laughed nervously.

Leland's cell rang. He just looked at it for a beat like he was deciding whether to answer. Then he did.

"Leland," he said annoyed. "Yeah," he listened. "Did they check the hotels?" paused, "Okay, keep me informed."

He hung up and looked at me.

"What'd I do now?"

"Not you this time. There's a Veterinarian missing in Marathon Key. His car is parked in front of his office and the door is unlocked, but no Doc."

"Eric and Olivia?"

"Could be. I'm going to send someone down there to keep an eye on it."

"Let me know. I need to keep a count on my enemies."

"Do you need anything before I go?"

"If you don't mind, would you ask the nurse to bring me a glass of milk," I said pointing at the sack.

"Will do."

Chapter 50

Eric's bleeding had stopped and he was feeling a little better.

"Good job, Doc," he said.

"It won't last," he said. "You need to go to the hospital."

"I will when I get to Miami."

"What about my leg?" Oliva said. "It still hurts like hell."

"You have a broken kneecap," he said. "You're not going to get any better until you have surgery."

"Fuck, fuck, fuck!" she yelled and started crying. "We had it all figured out but that damn Emily and Cam. I'll kill them."

"We're not going to worry about killing anyone. We need to figure out how to get out of here," Eric said.

He parted the blinds slightly to check the parking lot. He dropped them quickly when he saw a police cruiser slowly driving past.

"Shit, it's the cops," he said.

Emily sat up, "What now?"

Eric pulled his gun out of his belt, "Okay Doc, get in that closet and don't make a sound. I swear I'll put a bullet right through that door."

He pulled the Doctor up and pushed him toward the closet.

"Olivia, get your bra off and get under the sheets and put a big smile on your face."

Eric undressed but kept on his T-shirt to hide the bandage. He could hear the police knocking on the room door next to theirs.

"They're checking all the rooms," he said and handed Olivia the gun. "Put this under the sheets and use it if you have to."

The knock came on their door.

"Just a second," Eric called.

He picked up a towel and held it loosely in front of him as he opened the door.

"Can I help you?"

The officer looked at him in his obvious state of undress and then in the room where Olivia was lying in bed, one naked breast peeking out from under the sheet.

Eric let the towel slip slightly revealing he was also naked.

"Sorry to bother you," the officer said clearly embarrassed.

"That's okay," Olivia giggled, "You wanna join us?"

"No ma'am," he said tipping his hat. "We're just checking the rooms for a fugitive," he said sticking his head in the room and taking a quick look.

"You can come in and check under the sheets if you want," she said and laughed.

"Bridgett!" Eric said over his shoulder. "Sorry officer."

"Sorry to bother you, folks," the officer said and turned away.

Eric closed the door but didn't move until he heard the knock on the room next door.

"Very good, baby," he said.

Her smile faded and the pained look returned to her face.

"We need to leave tonight," Eric said.

Olivia pointed at the closet and raised her shoulders in a question.

Eric pulled his finger across his throat in answer.

Eric led the doctor back to the recliner. "Just get comfortable for a while," he said. "We're leaving here tonight but I want you to change our bandages again before we do."

"Then what?" the Doc said. "You gonna kill me?"

"No, but I am sorry we're going to have to tie you up. The cleaning lady will find you in the morning and we'll be long gone."

The doctor didn't believe that for a minute.

~***~

Diane and Kailey spent the evening in my room until I finally ran them out. I was tired and wanted to go over all the questions that have been going through my head.

Olivia and Eric would be found. I don't think they are a threat to any of us now but I want them to pay for what they've done.

Olan, on the other hand, is a big threat. How did he know the raid was about to take place and clearly by his gesture on the canal, he knows I killed his brother. Not to mention, he's already put a hit on me.

I saw Sergeant Jackson relieve the officer guarding my room. He stuck his head in the room. "Hey, Cam," he said. "You need anything?"

"No thanks. I'm good. The Doctor said I'll be out of here tomorrow."

"Great news. If you need anything I'll be right here."

"Thanks."

I closed my eyes and tried to sleep but my mind wouldn't let me. There was something that kept nagging me. Then my eyes flew open. I know what it is.

Two hours later, I heard my door open and an orderly stepped into the room. Jackson closed the door behind him.

He didn't look the type to be working in a hospital. Other than a white coat, he was too tan and large. His black hair was slicked back and he had a ponytail.

The revelation had just rung true. Jackson was on Chastain's payroll too. He's the one who tipped off Olan before the raid. The phone calls he made outside Olan's house allowing him to escape.

The orderly moved closer to the bed.

"Can I help you?" I said.

He reached under his jacket and pulled out a long knife. "Olan wanted me to give this to you," he said. "He knows you killed his brother. Tell Sly, "Hello" from Olan when you see him."

He raised the knife and I pulled the trigger. The man jerked back with a surprised look on his face. He looked down at his chest and then back at me. Then he fell to the floor.

The door flew open and Jackson entered the room, gun in hand.

He looked at the man on the floor then at me. He paused then pointed the gun at me. I fired again.

Jackson lay on the floor next to the orderly. I looked out the door expecting nurses to run into the room but the floor seemed deserted. Where was everyone?

Then Olan stepped into the room.

Chapter 51

"Let's go Doc," Eric said. "Get back in the closet."

"You're not going to tie me up," he asked panic in his voice.

"We won't need to."

The doctor turned and kicked out hitting Eric in his wound with the side of his foot. Eric fell to the floor in pain.

Olivia raised the gun and fired hitting the Doctor in the chest.

"Shit," she said. "Someone will have heard that shot. We have to get out of here now."

Eric lay on the floor holding his side. His shirt was already soaked in blood.

"Get up damn it," she said, "Let's go."

He got on his knees and used the bed to push himself up.

He helped Olivia hop to the car, got in and started the engine.

We'll get help when we get to Miami," he said.

Eric drove north on Highway 1 toward Miami. He put his hand to his side and felt the wet blood that was soaking his shirt.

Olivia was lying in the back seat crying. Her leg was getting worse and the pain was unbearable.

"You fucker," she spat. "You were going to blow me up in that house, weren't you?"

"Shut up," he said. "You told Cam where I was and he almost killed me. He got Kailey out before the house blew. Besides, I saved you now."

"What are we going to do?" she asked. "We still have the money from the last book and the house in Colorado no one knows about."

"That's where I'm headed," Eric said. "But I can't take the chance that you won't open your big mouth and tell someone about it."

"Fuck you," she said. "I was being tortured."

Eric turned off 1 onto an overgrown trail just south of Islamorada.

"Where are we going?" Olivia said.

"I have to stop the bleeding or I'll pass out," Eric said.

He drove to the end of the trail and stopped the car killing the lights.

Walking around to the back door, he opened it and told Olivia to get out.

"I can't," she said. "My leg has gotten worse."

Eric grabbed her foot and pulled her out of the car. She yelled in agony as she fell to the ground.

"You son of a bitch," she cried.

"You gotta stop my bleeding," he yelled.

He took off his shirt and then his blood-soaked T-shirt. He sat down next to Olivia and handed her the T-shirt.

"Wrap this around me, tight," he said.

She did. "How we going to fix my leg?" she said hoarsely.

"I'll adjust the splint and give you another sedative," he said.

She finished wrapping him up and tied the ends together so it would stay on.

"You need to keep pressure on that," she said. "Maybe we can find a drug store and get more bandages."

Eric reached in the front seat and picked up his gun.

"Sorry babe, but I can't take you with me."

Olivia's eyes widened as he pointed the gun at her head.

'Fuck you," she said and spat in his face.

Eric shot her and she died instantly.

He was getting weaker and knew he had to get help or he'd bleed out.

He started the car and turned it around. Halfway through the maneuver, the tire spun and the car sunk up to the axles instantly. He rocked the car back and forth trying to get out of the hole but only managed to throw mud and sink deeper.

"Mother fucker!" he yelled beating the steering wheel.

He got out and assessed the damage. The car was not going anywhere.

He looked back at Olivia one last time but felt nothing. He's wanted to get rid of that controlling bitch for a long time.

He started walking the quarter mile back to Highway 1. It was dark and he was weak. He imagined he heard all sorts of sounds coming from beside the trail in the darkness. No telling what was watching him from their hidey-holes.

When his legs were jerked from under him, he knew he wasn't imagining them any longer.

The alligator dragged him, kicking and screaming, into the swampy water only ten feet away.

Chapter 52

"Good evening, Cam," Olan said.

"Olan," I nodded. "Have you come to see how I am?"

"No, I know how you are."

He looked at the floor where the two men lay dead.

"You've been busy. Leland's going to be pissed," he said.

"I doubt it."

He smiled and reached inside his coat pulling out a 357 magnum. He then reached in his other pocket and revealed a silencer and began to screw it on the gun.

"So," I said. "Jackson was working for you."

"Yes, I'm afraid I'll have to replace him now," he said looking down at him again.

"And Leland?"

Olan looked at me his smile broadening. "How did you figure that out?"

"Well, first, he tried to talk us out of raiding your house."

"I wondered if he did."

"Then, he wouldn't help Dave when he came to him. The next clue was because of me. I told him where Dave was and he told you."

"Very good," Olan said.

"And you always seem to get off scott free."

"Well, that's because I never do any of those things I'm accused of," he said shrugging his shoulders.

"You don't?" I said sarcastically.

"It's time for you to die, Cam."

I pulled the gun out from under the sheets for him to see.

He smiled again not bothering to aim his gun yet.

"Go ahead and shoot, Cam."

"I don't think you want me to do that."

"Sure, why not," he said. "I know something you don't know."

"Really? I think I know something you don't know I know."

His smile faded a little.

"Leland said he always carries a nine-millimeter, but I've noticed he carries a forty-five so I checked the clip he gave me. Can you believe it? It only had two bullets in it. One for each of the sacrificial lambs there on the floor. He knew someone would give me my gun so why not him?"

I pulled my other hand out from under the bed and showed him the clip Leland had given me.

Olan stood still not raising his gun. I could tell he was contemplating his next move. Then he smiled again.

"Okay, Cam. You win this round since you have a gun aimed at my chest. I'll be back though and I'll find you and I'll kill you. I'll see you around," he said turning to leave.

Sheriff Rogers and two deputies were blocking the door.

"Ya goin' somewhere Olan?" Rogers said.

"Move sheriff or you'll pay the price."

"What would that price be?"

Olan looked at one of the deputies and said, "Paul?"

The deputy pulled his gun and put it to the sheriff's head.

"What the fuck?" Rogers said.

"I warned you, sheriff," Olan said.

I still had my gun aimed at Olan but I wasn't going to shoot him in the back. On the other hand, I can't let them kill Sheriff Rogers either. A dilemma.

Olan turned toward me again. "I have plenty of help in high places, Cam. You'll be dead in twenty-four hours."

The sheriff and his deputies backed out of the room slowly, the gun still pointed at Rogers's head. I heard a gunshot and chaos erupted.

To my surprise, the deputy with the gun fell to the floor. Then there was another shot and Olan flew backward, hit the bed and fell face down beside Jackson.

The sheriff and other deputy were frozen in their tracks. Finally, they turned to see who had killed these men. They parted and Kailey walked into the room.

"You okay, Cam?" she asked dropping her gun on the floor.

"I'm fine, come here."

I patted the bed next to me and Kailey lay down.

Sheriff Rogers and Deputy Fallon stood in the doorway staring at us.

"They're all yours sheriff," I said. "The way I see it Kailey just saved your lives. After she killed the deputy, who was about to kill you, there could be no other outcome, she shot Olan who was raising his gun toward you."

They still stood just looking at us. Finally, Rogers said, "I'll call this in."

"Did you get all of it on tape?" I asked.

"Yep," Rogers said. "It was just like you said it would be. We'll pick Leland up as soon as we leave here."

They turned to leave and stopped. Turning around Rogers said, "Good work Kailey. I owe you a big one."

The place was swarming with police and FBI in a matter of an hour.

Kailey was still lying in bed with me.

"Did you have to kill Olan?" I asked her.

"He would have never let you live," she said. "One way or the other he would have ordered your hit. I couldn't allow that."

"You're right. I was already trying to figure out how I was going to get rid of him."

"Sometimes you just gotta kill 'em, Cam," she said.

"Yes, a famous author once told me that."

"Yes, I heard him."

Chapter 53

We sat on the lanai drinking Wild Turkey and eating chocolate honey buns, Diane, Jack, Stacy, Barbie, Cody, Kailey and me. Hank was eating treats and Walter was gnawing on a big Porterhouse bone.

"We should live every day like the first or the last one," I said raising my glass.

That got a round of "Yeahs" from the group.

This was my first day out of the hospital and we were celebrating life.

My cell rang. I looked at it vibrating around the table wondering if I should answer or not.

"You better get it, Cam," Kailey said.

"Hello?" I answered.

I listened for a minute and said, "Great. Don't let him out of the house for a few days. You know how he gets." Pause, "Okay, have fun. Goodbye."

I picked up my drink and took a swallow.

Eight sets of eyes were staring at me if you count Walter and Hank.

"What?" I said.

"Who was that?" voices were saying.

"Crazy Wanda. She said Angelo Perez's men dropped Dave off a few minutes ago. Dave said Chastain's men tied him to a post in a warehouse. They were going to cut him up and feed him to the fishes. Suddenly Perez's men rushed in guns blazing and killed all of them. Then they untied Dave and said, "Would you like a ride home?"

Everyone sat silent and then burst into laughter.

"Only Dave," Diane said.

"What's so funny?" a voice said from behind us.

We turned to see Emily standing at the entrance.

"Come aboard," I said.

She sat at the table and Kailey fixed her a drink.

"We were just cheering our old friend Dave who came back from the dead," Diane said.

"Well, here's to Dave," Emily said raising her glass.

"To Dave," everyone harmonized.

"I didn't expect to see you again," I said.

"I was in the neighborhood. Did you know that Chief Leland is no longer with the police department?"

"Yes, we heard about that," I said.

After a beat, she said, "They found Olivia."

"Good, maybe she'll give up Eric and they can settle that case."

"I'm afraid she can't give anyone up. She was murdered."

"Murdered?" Cody said.

"Eric shot her. They killed a Veterinarian in Marathon also."

We exchanged looks around the table shaking our heads.

"They didn't find Eric," Emily said, "but there was a blood trail leading from their car where he shot Olivia. It looks like maybe an alligator drug Eric away."

"Okay, I'll take that," Cody said.

"To the alligator," Stacy said raising her glass.

We all hesitated looking at one another.

"What the hell," I said.

"To the alligator," we all said toasting.

Cody went home two days later; he said he was going to rethink his books. Maybe take out some of the more gruesome parts.

"Don't let them beat you, Cody. Be yourself. None of this was your fault," I said.

"Maybe your right, Cam. It always worked for me before, but every time I kill someone now I'll see it really happening. I hope I can get past that."

"Hell, Cody," I said. "Sometimes you just gotta kill 'em."

Epilogue

Eight days later, I flew Kailey back to Aspen. We had spent a great week, mostly in bed. I couldn't get enough of her.

I stayed in Aspen for two weeks in her humble mansion.

We were eating at the French Alpine Bistro. Kailey had the Black & Wild. Wild mushrooms in white sauce, topped with freshly shaved black truffle. I was having Escargots en Brioche sautéed with garlic butter, tomato concassée, Pastis, and toasted brioche.

I held up my glass of Philippe Colin Clos Saint-Jean 2015 and toasted. "To the most beautiful woman in all the world. My protector, my angle, my love and someday, my wife."

We clicked our glasses together.

"Someday I will be thrilled to have you for my husband. But for now, I still have some work to do on my temper."

"If it weren't for your temper, I might be dead right now," I said.

"I would never let that happen. I'll always be there, even when you don't know I'm there."

I thought about that. It was true. She is always there. Sometimes in my house and sometimes even in my bed when I don't know it. But, you know what? I don't care. I might be a big tough private eye, but it's refreshing to know there is someone looking out for *me*.

THE END

Books by Mac Fortner:

<u>On Amazon:</u>

Knee Deep
Bloodshot
Key West: Two Birds One Stone
Murder Fest Key West

Rum City Bar
Battle For Rumora

FREE NOVELLA: PREQUEL TO THE CAM DERRINGER SERIES:

<u>A DARK NIGHT IN KEY WEST</u>

https://bit.ly/2JRAFEX

Mac Fortner

MURDER FEST KEY WEST

Made in the USA
Middletown, DE
20 September 2020